# TRAPPING THE BEAST

A sound outside brought them both to their feet; the unmistakable *snap* of metal jaws clamping together. Then came a roar such as no beast ever mouthed, a roar like thunder, an outburst of agony and rage that echoed off the mountains and rolled out across the plain below the foothills.

"It worked! The trap got it!" Shakespeare McNair exclaimed. "I'll finish it off while we have the chance!" As he reached for the latch they heard another roar—much closer to the cabin.

"Don't go out there!" Blue Water Woman shouted.

Shakespeare hesitated.

Then, through the door, came heavy, labored breaths. Something scraped against the wood. Blue Water Woman ran to her rifle. Cocking the hammer, she turned as a hideous growl replaced the breathing.

"I forgot the brace!" Shakespeare cried. The stout oak branch was leaning against the wall, and he hurriedly wedged it against the bar. He leaped back just as the door was battered by a fierce blow. The repaired hinge held but the entire door vibrated.

Blue Water Woman ran to his side. A second blow landed. A third. When each landed there was a heavy *thunk,* almost as if the creature's claws were tearing into the wood.

"Did you hear that?" Shakespear exclaimed. "It's using our axe! The thing is chopping its way inside!"

The *Wilderness* Series:

**#1: KING OF THE MOUNTAIN**
**#2: LURE OF THE WILD**
**#3: SAVAGE RENDEZVOUS**
**#4: BLOOD FURY**
**#5: TOMAHAWK REVENGE**
**#6: BLACK POWDER JUSTICE**
**#7: VENGEANCE TRAIL**
**#8: DEATH HUNT**
**#9: MOUNTAIN DEVIL**
**#10: BLACKFOOT MASSACRE**
**#11: NORTHWEST PASSAGE**
**#12: APACHE BLOOD**
**#13: MOUNTAIN MANHUNT**
**#14: TENDERFOOT**
**#15: WINTERKILL**
**#16: BLOOD TRUCE**
**#17: TRAPPER'S BLOOD**
**#18: MOUNTAIN CAT**
**#19: IRON WARRIOR**
**#20: WOLF PACK**
**#21: BLACK POWDER**
**#22: TRAIL'S END**
**#23: THE LOST VALLEY**
**#24: MOUNTAIN MADNESS**
**#25: FRONTIER MAYHEM**
**#26: BLOOD FEUD**
**#27: GOLD RAGE**
**#28: THE QUEST**
**#29: MOUNTAIN NIGHTMARE**
**#30: SAVAGES**
**#31: BLOOD KIN**
**#32: THE WESTWARD TIDE**
**#33: FANG AND CLAW**
**#34: TRACKDOWN**
**#35: FRONTIER FURY**

# WILDERNESS
# The Tempest

# David Thompson

**LEISURE BOOKS**  NEW YORK CITY

*Dedicated to Judy, Joshua and Shane.*

A LEISURE BOOK®

April 2002

Published by

Dorchester Publishing Co., Inc.
276 Fifth Avenue
New York, NY 10001

ISBN 0-8439-4992-9

Printed in the United States of America.

Visit us on the web at www.dorchesterpub.com.

# The Tempest

# *Chapter One*

Slate-gray clouds hung lifeless in the sky like bodies on a mist-shrouded battlefield. Gloom mired the Rocky Mountains, and more than the bleak weather was to blame. Normally, birds would be chirping and chipmunks would be chittering, but on this particular morning the wilderness was extraordinarily still.

Shakespeare McNair did not like it one bit. He was of average height and size and radiated robust health rare for a man in his eighties. All the friends of his youth had long since succumbed to the scythe of the Reaper, but not him. Often younger mountain men asked how it was he had lived so long, and he always honestly replied he had no idea. Diet wasn't a factor; Shakespeare had an exceptional fondness for fatty foods, sugar, and coffee that by rights should have done in him long ago. Nor did long-lived people run in his family. His own father had died at the age of forty-one of heart problems, his mother at thirty from pneumonia.

The best Shakespeare could figure, his vigorous way of life was responsible for his longevity. For more years than any other white man he had called the Rocky Mountains home. Each and every day, without fail, had been filled with nonstop activity. From dawn until dusk he was always on the go, always working at this or that. Always being on the go and having things to do had kept him slim and healthy and lent him a vitality men half his age envied.

Shakespeare's shoulder-length hair and long beard were white as snow. He had large, ruddy cheeks, and when he smiled, he displayed a mouth brimming with healthy teeth, which was more than many of his fellow mountaineers could say. Usually, his lake-blue eyes held a playful twinkle, but on this grim and dreary morning Shakespeare's eyes were troubled. He didn't like it when the wildlife went quiet. It was always a bad sign, for it always happened when a predator was abroad, and not necessarily a four-legged predator, either.

Hefting the ax he had brought from his cabin to chop wood, Shakespeare moved toward a pile of pines he had felled a month before, before the weather turned cold. He wore beaded buckskins made by his Flathead wife, Blue Water Woman. Slanted across his chest were a powder horn and ammo pouch. On his left hip hung a Green River knife. Tucked under the front of his wide brown leather belt was a flintlock pistol. He had left his Hawken rifle inside and considered going back for it, but he dismissed his nervousness as the result of too much imagination fueled by too much coffee.

Still, Shakespeare kept his eyes and ears primed. In the Rockies a man never knew from one second to the next when he might be beset by savage beasts or roving hostiles. Not to mention the occasional bands of white cutthroats who had been showing up in the mountains in increased numbers in recent years.

"They with continual action are even as good as rotten," Shakespeare muttered at the thought. As was his habit, he was quoting his namesake, the famed Bard of Avalon. In his cabin, on a prized spot on the stone mantel, sat Shakespeare's well-

2

worn copy of *The Complete Works of William Shakespeare*. He knew it from end to end and could quote whole passages by the hour. For that reason his trapping peers of long ago had bestowed his nickname, and he'd liked it so much he had adopted it as his own and forever after introduced himself as "Shakespeare" McNair.

Now Shakespeare suited the bard to his notions about the new breed by paraphrasing, "Thou art all knaves and rascals, eaters of broken meats, base, proud, shallow, beggarly, three-suited, hundred-pound, filthy worsted stocking scoundrels. You're all lily-livered whoresons and I spit on you." With that, Shakespeare spat, and chuckled at his own humor.

The pile of downed trees was twenty yards south of the cabin. As he planted himself and gripped the long ax handle firmly with both hands, Shakespeare glanced at his sturdily built home, at the smoke curling lazily from the chimney and the few hardy flowers still in bloom in his wife's small garden. They had been living there for nigh on two decades. Without question, it had been one of the happiest periods of his entire life.

Shakespeare swung the ax and the keen edge bit deep into a log. Chips went flying. He repeated the motion, always chopping at a precise angle to more quickly shear through the wood. He had taken about eight or nine swings when the short hairs at the nape of his neck prickled. Instantly he turned, his right hand dropping to the smooth butt of his pistol.

*Something was watching him.* Shakespeare trusted his instincts implicitly. Honed by hard experience and bitter necessity, they had saved his hide and hair many a time. Something was out there, all right. Something that had driven all the peaceful creatures that always frolicked unconcerned nearby into hiding.

"I like it not," Shakespeare said, and gave a little start when the latch to the front door rasped loudly in the stillness and his wife stepped outside.

"Care for some help carrying in the firewood, husband?" Blue Water Woman asked in English.

# David Thompson

Shakespeare turned. As it had every day since they first met, the sight of her, standing there so beautiful and serene, stirred him heart and soul. A beaded buckskin dress clung to her still-youthful body. Her oval face bore wrinkles but nowhere near as many as his, and she had long raven tresses sprinkled with gray. Her most prominent feature were deep, dark, lovely eyes, which were aglow with affection. "I care for my rifle, wench," he said, his tone sufficient to indicate why.

Blue Water Woman cast a quick glance at the surrounding woodland. "Right away." She ducked back inside.

No questions about why. No carping comments to the effect that if he needed it so much, he could get it himself. Blue Water Woman was remarkably free of a trait Shakespeare had observed in most others of her gender—namely, the tendency to question, nag, and complain until it drove most men to distraction. Yet another reason he loved her so.

Blue Water Woman reappeared, holding her Hawken as well as his. Their rifles were always kept propped against the front wall near the door, ready for immediate use. "Here you go," she said, hurrying over.

Shakespeare grinned and recited, " 'O, she doth teach the torches to burn bright! It seems she hangs upon the cheek of night like a rich jewel in an Ethiop's ear. Beauty too rich for use, for earth too dear!' "

Blue Water Woman tilted her head back to survey the sky. "It's daytime, not night. And if we were rich, I would have you build me a great stone house like those we saw in St. Louis."

"Damn you, woman," Shakespeare said. "I'm waxing romantic and you prick me with your rapier tongue."

They laughed, and Shakespeare set down the ax and took his heavy rifle. "How about a stroll, my dear?"

"Only if you promise to keep your hands to yourself," Blue Water Woman said. "I know how randy you are in the morning."

Shakespeare laughed anew, uproariously. In his younger days

he had known some prim white gals who wouldn't use words like "randy" for fear of being struck dead by a lightning bolt hurled from above by a wrathful Creator. "You sure are a caution. And since you've brought it up, honor requires I mention that you've never pushed me away when I'm feeling a mite frisky. Morning or otherwise."

"A woman is obligated to let her man have his way," Blue Water Woman held her own. "If for no other reason than to put him in a good mood so he won't grumble so much."

"When do men grumble?" Shakespeare demanded. "We're daisies from toenails to follicles. It's you women who claim first honors when it comes to nitpicking."

Blue Water Woman's smile was as sweet as it was deceptive. "If I were a nitpicker, I would never have married a man who won't clean up after himself and whose idea of washing dishes is to leave them outside until it rains."

Shakespeare headed toward the trees, the Hawken cradled at his hip. "Hell, minx. Until I came along, you didn't use dishes. You ate out of a big pot with your hands, remember? Or put the food on bark plates."

"Are you saying I was uncivilized?" Blue Water Woman inquired in a not quite so playful manner.

The moment of triumph was sweet. Shakespeare snickered and said, "Only in bed, my darling. Only in bed."

A pink tinge suffused Blue Water Woman's cheeks. "You are a lustful rogue," she said softly.

"And you love it," Shakespeare teased. "Now hush, will you? A silvertip could sneak up on us and we'd never know it with all our jabbering." His wife dutifully fell silent. She was no pampered, witless easterner, fresh off a wagon train, the kind who blundered through the wilds like a blind ox waiting for slaughter. She was a full-blooded Flathead, raised in a culture where violence and warfare were a constant part of life. When she was little, her village had been raided three times, twice by Blackfeet and once by Bloods. She had seen kin and friends massacred.

She had learned to always be vigilant, to always tread lightly and keep her ears perked.

The scuttling gray clouds lent a preternatural twilight to the landscape, shrouding the forest in pale gloom. Shakespeare stopped to scour the vegetation, probing shadows and thickets, his thumb on the Hawken's hammer.

"We are being watched, husband," Blue Water Woman whispered.

Shakespeare nodded. The feeling was stronger than ever, like a heat rash no amount of scratching would relieve. On an impulse he roved to the left along the tree line, toward a stream that meandered along the border of the broad clearing their cabin dominated. A breeze was blowing, stiff enough to rustle the leaves of some aspens Shakespeare passed. He scanned the ground for tracks, the brush for signs of recent passage, for freshly broken twigs or crushed blades of grass.

Shakespeare heard the stream before he saw it, heard the soft gurgling of swiftly flowing water over the multitude of rocks that littered the bed. He halted on the low bank. Less than a foot deep, the stream ran year-round, runoff from the snow-crowned peaks to the west. Their cabin was situated near a sharp bend. At the point he was standing, the waterway diverted from a generally easterly course to the south. He surveyed its length but saw nothing to account for his persistent unease.

"Look there!" Blue Water Woman said, pointing.

Shakespeare glanced down at the soft soil at the water's edge, and his breath caught in his throat. Clearly imprinted in the dank earth was a footprint unlike any he had ever seen. Hopping off the bank, he hunkered down to examine it. The length, he estimated, was twenty inches, far longer than any human's. Longer, even, than those of the largest grizzlies. The general shape, though, was quite bearlike except for the heel, which was much too broad. Even stranger, it had distinct humanlike toes that ended in long points. Shakespeare might still be inclined to believe a bear was responsible were it not for the fact the small toe was on the outside of the track; in bears, the small toe was always on the inside.

Blue Water Woman crouched for a better look. "I have never seen such a print. What kind of animal could have made it?"

"I wish I knew," Shakespeare said. He remembered a story told by his close friend, Nate King, who once had a run-in with huge, hairy creatures that walked on two legs and left gigantic footprints exactly like those of men. The description Nate gave of their tracks, though, didn't match the print in front of him. "Maybe it's the critter Canadians call a mammoth," he speculated. In the hinterland of the far north existed a beast of legend early trappers had called by that name, a beast so elusive few ever saw its tracks. Rumor had it that anyone who saw the actual beast never lived to tell the tale.

"A mammoth this far south?" Blue Water Woman said skeptically.

Shakespeare touched a fingertip to the impression. "Whatever it is, it sure as hell is something." The earth was soft, the texture fine. The track had been made that very morning, less than an hour before, if he was any judge. "And whatever it is, it must be real close."

Blue Water Woman rose. "That explains the feeling I have."

And his, Shakespeare thought. Straightening, he roved in search of more bizarre footprints and found a partial print on the bank where the creature had stepped up out of the stream and gone off into the trees. Despite its size it had a knack for treading lightly, and he failed to find another complete track although he went over fifty yards. He did find a few short black hairs stuck to a prickly bush. They resembled a black bear's, but he couldn't reconcile them with the tracks.

Stymied, Shakespeare returned to the stream to backtrack the thing. Smudge marks indicated it had come from the north, stepped down off the bank to drink, then gone on into the woods.

"Maybe the creature is waiting for a chance to jump us," Blue

# David Thompson

Water Woman said. "Like that mountain lion two winters ago."

A big painter had come down from the high country in the fall. Old, past its prime, the cat had been unable to bring down deer and other game and had lain in ambush for Blue Water Woman one evening as she was toting water to the cabin. Only the fact that Shakespeare had spotted it when it slunk up on her from behind had saved her from being severely hurt, or worse. He'd had his rifle with him and shot it as it sprang.

"We'll have to keep our eyes skinned," his wife remarked.

"We'll have to do more than that," Shakespeare said. He couldn't—he wouldn't—abide any threat to his beloved. "I reckon I'll lay a little trap for the critter after I'm done chopping logs."

"I will stand guard," Blue Water Woman offered. "We need the firewood. Cold weather is moving in, and we might have an early snow before the week is out."

Shakespeare never ceased to be amazed by her knack for predicting the weather. At the moment the temperature was in the upper forties, and other than the low, scuttling clouds, there was no hint of an impending change. "Are your knuckles aching again?"

"Yes."

His wife's hands were remarkably sensitive; any abrupt change in the weather and they plagued her something awful. There were times it got so bad she could barely move her fingers. Shakespeare had tried every poultice and remedy he could think of or had ever heard about, but they failed to help. "I'd best cut up a lot of logs, then, huh?" he said without much enthusiasm. He'd been hoping to get by with an armload.

Blue Water Woman smiled. "The exercise will do you good. You do not get as much as you used to."

"At my age I'm lucky if I can get out of bed in the morning," Shakespeare said. "When you think about it, old as I am, I should have a wife who waits on me hand and foot."

"Want me to find you a new woman?" Blue Water Woman

asked, unruffled. "Someone younger, perhaps? And gullible enough to believe everything you say?"

Shakespeare sighed. "If not for my iron constitution, your barbs would have reduced me to a frazzle a coon's age ago."

"If not for your silly posturing, I would have much less to laugh at."

Conceding victory, Shakespeare leaned over and pecked her on the cheek. "I'll say one thing. Life with you has never been dull."

Blue Water Woman touched his hand. "We were meant for each other, you and I."

Shakespeare tended to agree, although they would never have known it given how their lives turned out. He had met her ages ago, shortly after he initially came west. Typical of youthful, hot-blooded passion, they had fallen deeply in love and made plans to become man and wife. Then her father stepped in. Broken Feather disliked whites on general principle, and he forbade Blue Water Woman to have anything more to do with her white suitor. A dutiful daughter, she had sadly obeyed.

Devastated, Shakespeare pined for her for over a year. Eventually the hurt scarred over, as emotional hurts were wont to do, and he got on with his life. Much later he learned that Broken Feather had married her off to a prominent warrior, Spotted Owl. As for him, he met and married Rainbow Woman, a lovely Flathead from a different village.

Years passed. Rainbow Woman was slain by the Blackfeet in a raid. Spotted Owl died, leaving Blue Water Woman a widow. Fate conspired to bring Shakespeare and her together again, and they had been together ever since. Two decades of being as much in love as two people could be. Two decades of Shakespeare waking up every morning thankful to be lying next to the woman who had claimed his heart, lo those many summers ago.

Shakespeare's only regret was that they had been reunited too late in life to have children. Blue Water Woman shared the sentiment, for now and then, late at night when they were cuddled in each other's arms, she would mention how much she wished they had sons and daughters so she could hold their grandchildren on her lap and rock them to sleep beside the fireplace each evening.

Now, reaching the logs, Shakespeare leaned his rifle against them and bent to retrieve his ax. Only, it wasn't there. Puzzled, he looked right and left, but it was definitely gone. "That's peculiar," he said.

"What is?" Blue Water Woman had been studying the trees. Looking down, she asked, "What happened to your ax?"

"Maybe it sprouted wings and flew off." Shakespeare shifted around, and his blood ran cold a second time that morning. Imprinted in dirt next to the logs were more of the strange footprints. Whatever made them had made off with his ax while they were in the forest.

"I thought I shut the door when I came out," Blue Water Woman suddenly commented.

Shakespeare glanced at the front of their cabin. Sure enough, the door was wide open. Snatching up his Hawken, he cocked the hammer and cautiously advanced. His wife flanked him, her own weapon held rock-steady.

"Be careful. It can't be an animal."

Shakespeare was thinking the same thing. A bear might help itself to the deer meat he had drying on a rack. It might rip apart their bench or root in the garden. But no bear—or any other wild beast—would steal an ax.

Pausing at the jamb, Shakespeare strained his ears but heard nothing out of the ordinary. He noticed scratch marks high on the door, five furrows such as claws would make. Tucking the Hawken's stock to his shoulder, he stepped into the doorway, ready to fire at anything that moved.

"Look!" Blue Water Woman cried.

The interior was a mess. The cupboard doors were open and foodstuffs had been strewn wildly about. Their sugar and flour had splashed over the floor and walls. Their table had been upended and the bearskin rug on which it had sat had been thrown into a corner. A towel that had been hanging on a peg by the washbasin had been torn in half. A few cooking utensils had been taken from a drawer and bent in half. A doll that belonged to Blue Water Woman when she was little had been removed from the mantel and dropped near the rocker, one arm ripped off.

Shakespeare's favorite pipe, which he always left beside the doll, was on the floor, snapped in half. "Bastard!" he said, picking up the pieces. "Methink'st thou art a general offense and every man should beat thee."

"So you believe it is a man after all?"

"I don't know what to believe." Shakespeare turned toward a door recessed in the right-hand wall. His wife had always insisted on having a bedroom, like the Kings, so some time back he had invited Nate up for a visit and when Nate arrived handed him a saw and hammer. It took them two whole weeks to put on the addition. At the moment the door was shut; maybe, just maybe, the intruder was still in there.

Motioning to Blue Water Woman, Shakespeare touched a finger to his lips, then catfooted over and placed an ear to the pine. He didn't hear any sounds, but that didn't mean a thing. Slowly, every nerve jangling, Shakespeare gripped the latch. Girding himself, he flung the door inward and jerked the Hawken to his shoulder. But there was nothing to shoot. Their bedroom was undisturbed, every article exactly as it should be.

"What's that odor, husband?"

Shakespeare pivoted. Now that she mentioned it, there was a foul smell in the air, faint but pervasive. It reminded him of a bear den right after bears emerged from hibernation, a sickly-sweet yet undeniably awful stench, fit to gag a goat.

"We must air the place out," Blue Water Woman said, moving to open the windows. Like Winona, Nate King's wife, she'd wanted real glass, not hide or burlap covers. An exorbitant expense, in Shakespeare's opinion, but he had never been able to say no to her, so one spring he'd made a special trip to St. Louis just to obtain a few panes.

"It can't have gotten far," Shakespeare said, hastening to the entrance. "I'm going to look for more sign."

"I'll come with you," Blue Water Woman volunteered.

"I can manage. Why don't you start cleaning up this mess?" Shakespeare was outside before she could object. Truth was, his unease had grown. Whatever was skulking about their place was stealthier than a wolf and slyer than a fox. And incredibly huge. He'd rather confront it on his own.

Shakespeare circled the cabin. At the northwest corner a line of clear prints led into the woods. The creature possessed an ungodly long stride, covering four feet at a single step. Shakespeare broke into a jog, thinking to overtake it before it went too far. But after a hundred yards he slowed, aware of the futility of his attempt.

On reaching the edge of a clearing, Shakespeare halted to catch his breath. He wasn't as spry as he used to be, and the run had left him a bit winded. Raising a sleeve to wipe his brow, he saw an object that glinted dully in the tall grass. He couldn't quite make out what it was, but he assumed it must be his missing ax, and raising the Hawken, he advanced.

"Well, I'll be," Shakespeare breathed. He was wrong. It was their fireplace poker, which he hadn't realized the intruder had taken. Bending, he picked it up, and his entire body broke out in goose bumps.

The poker had been bent into a U. Whatever had taken it had twisted the thick, heavy-gauge iron as if it were wax. Leaning his rifle against his side, Shakespeare tried to straighten the poker but couldn't unbend it a fraction. The strength required was prodigious. Not even a grizzly could perform such a feat. Which begged the question: What had?

Shakespeare's mind filled with tales and legends he had heard from the Indians over the years, accounts by the Flatheads, Shoshones, Nez Percé and others of huge beasts that once roamed the mountains and prairies and, some claimed, still dwelled in remote stretches of the Rockies where no man ever set foot. "This just can't be," he said aloud, lowering the poker.

Then Shakespeare saw it. A quarter mile away, climbing a sparsely wooded slope, was a dark, lumbering shape. With the swiftness of thought he dropped the poker and brought up his Hawken, but he didn't shoot. The thing was too far off. Squinting, he tried to distinguish details. As best he could tell, the creature was undeniably huge and hairy. It moved with an odd rolling gait similar to that of a silvertip, yet not quite the same. Rare fear rippled through him, not for himself but for his wife. Whatever the creature was, it might see fit to pay them another visit. Perhaps when he wasn't there.

Thinking to trick it into turning around, Shakespeare cupped a hand to his mouth and cut loose with a war whoop. He waited, holding his breath, and after a second the thing stopped and swiveled. All he saw was a dark, formless *thing* with no limbs to speak of, and no head, either.

"This just can't be," Shakespeare repeated.

As if to contradict him, the creature reared upward, swelling in size, and on the breeze wavered a piercing cry, part roar, part screech, part guttural rumble, the likes of which Shakespeare had never heard. Taking a few steps, he raised an arm and hollered in frustration, "What *are* you?"

The thing on the slope stared down at him a bit. Then it turned and resumed climbing.

Within seconds the verdant forest canopy swallowed the dark mass, and Shakespeare McNair involuntarily shuddered.

# Chapter Two

Blue Water Woman prided herself on two things. Foremost was her wise decision to take Carcajou, as McNair was known to her people, to be her mate. Second was her ability to stay calm when danger loomed. In times of crisis, when others around her were in a panic, she always managed to maintain her composure—a trait she demonstrated when she had barely seen seven winters, on the day Bloods raided her village. Many of the women and children had been running about in mindless fright, screaming and wailing, but not her. She'd had the presence of mind to grab her father's bow and quiver and rush outside to give it to him, then stood close by and watched as all around her warriors fought in fierce combat and people she knew and cared for were callously cut down. Eventually the Flatheads drove the invaders off, but at a terrible cost.

Her father had been impressed by her courage and bearing. Afterward he'd commented with pride to all who would listen that she had been as calm as the blue water of the tranquil lake near the village. From that day forth she was known as Blue

Water Woman. Many winters had gone by since, but in all that time she had never lost her inner calm, never let fear or anxiety rule her.

Until now.

Seven sleeps had gone by since their cabin was entered and ransacked. Initially, Blue Water Woman assumed that the creature would drift elsewhere, since large animals seldom stayed in one area for long. They roamed far and wide in search of forage or prey, and she figured the intruder would do the same. But she was wrong.

The second day, late in the evening, as Blue Water Woman sat in her rocker knitting and Shakespeare was cleaning his matched set of smoothbore pistols, an eerie cry rose from the surrounding forest. A ghastly shriek that seared into the core of her being and brought her out of the chair with a hand to her throat and her heart fluttering.

Shakespeare jumped up too, his face drained of color, and ran to the front door to unbar it.

"No!" Blue Water Woman had shouted. For a reason she couldn't comprehend, raw fear flooded through her, fear that if her man went out she would never see him again. "Wait until daylight and track it down."

There had been a time when Shakespeare would have laughed and stalked out anyway. But that night he let go of the long wooden bar and nodded. "Makes sense to me. Guess I wasn't thinking straight."

Blue Water Woman had seldom seen Carcajou scared. Concerned for her safety, yes. Afraid that she might be hurt, most assuredly. But never scared of anyone or anything. Yet that night she sensed fear in him, fear and something else. Shame. To ease his self-reproach she had joked, "Just like a man. Always ready to rush off to battle and leave us women on our own."

For a long time they had listened, but the unearthly cry wasn't repeated, and at their usual hour they turned in. As was Blue Water Woman's custom, she had molded her naked body to

15

his. Most nights he was soft and cuddly, but that night it had been like holding a board. He was still lying there tense and grim, his eyes wide open, when she finally dozed off.

The next day Shakespeare had gone out looking for sign, in vain. But the feeling that they were being watched persisted. She kept the curtains pulled even in broad daylight, and at night Shakespeare not only barred the door, he brought in a stout four-foot length of oak and wedged it against the bar for added bracing.

By mutual agreement neither ventured outside alone. The other was always on hand to stand guard. They never saw or heard anything out of the ordinary, but it unnerved them just the same.

Especially since all the wildlife had disappeared.

For days Blue Water Woman hadn't seen a single bird, which upset her considerably. She always liked to hear the sparrows chirp and the songbirds warble. The salt lick she had set out for the deer went unused, and a doe and fawn that had been coming around for weeks vanished.

Then, just the night before, after Shakespeare had blown out the lantern and they were about to undress, they had been startled by a tremendous thump on the rear wall. Shakespeare dashed to get his rifle. She'd grabbed a pair of pistols. Back-to-back they stood in the center of the main room, scarcely breathing, waiting for the thump to be repeated. And it was. A loud blow to the north wall dislodged caulking from between the logs. Another sent several of Shakespeare's books tumbling from a shelf.

"What *is* it?" Blue Water Woman had whispered.

"It sure isn't a bear," Shakespeare responded. He made no move to remove the bar, as he had that first night.

The thumping stopped. Blue Water Woman tried to soothe her frayed nerves, but she couldn't dispel an intense feeling of icy dread.

"If it breaks in," Shakespeare whispered, "run into the bedroom and push the bed and dresser against the door. I'll hold it off as long as I can."

"I will do no such thing," Blue Water Woman told him. "I am your wife. My place is at your side."

Shakespeare's teeth had shown white in the gloom. " 'Females! As contrary as the year is long.' " He quoted from his namesake. " 'Will not a calve's-skin stop that mouth of thine?' "

Blue Water Woman had lived with him for so long, had listened to him read aloud from his cherished book for countless hours on end, and been the brunt of so many quotes, that she could quote the Bard herself. "What folly I commit I dedicate to you."

Suddenly another blow struck the cabin. But this time, the front door bore the brunt. It resounded to the impact, violently shaking on its leather hinges.

"The creature is trying to break in!" Blue Water Woman had exclaimed.

Again the thing smashed the door, and the whole cabin seemed to shake. The bar and the stout branch bent but didn't give. The upper hinge, though, fared worse, the thick leather ripping partway through. The door sagged slightly, an inch-wide gap appearing at the very top.

"Enough of this!" Shakespeare declared. Moving closer, he pointed the muzzle of his Hawken at the center of the door and fired.

Blue Water Woman recoiled at the ear-blistering screech that resulted, a wail of hideous dimensions, torn from lungs that couldn't be remotely human. It was followed by a roar of pain and outrage that faded as its maker retreated into the night. So, too, faded the crackle of undergrowth, the crunch and snap of vegetation being torn asunder. In the terrible silence the creature left in its wake, she heard the wild hammering of her heart.

"So it can be hurt," Shakespeare had said with a grin. "And if it can be hurt, it can be killed. Tomorrow we're fighting back."

"How?" Blue Water Woman had asked.

"You'll see."

Now here they were, at the stream, Blue Water Woman with her rifle tucked under her arm, keeping watch while Shakespeare dug a shallow hole with a shovel. "I am not sure I like this idea," she commented. "We might only make the creature madder than it must already be."

"Serves it right," Shakespeare said without looking up. "The thing has us cowering under our blankets at night, like little children. I, for one, am mighty tired of being intimidated. If nothing else, we'll teach it to stop coming around."

Blue Water Woman glanced at a large metal trap near the hole, one of several Shakespeare intended to set. Easily ten times the size of a beaver trap, it was designed to hold bears—specifically, grizzly bears. Carcajou had them custom-made in St. Louis not all that long before after conventional traps failed to stop a young grizzly that made a serious nuisance of itself. Constructed of heavy-gauge steel, the springs and the jaws were two inches thick. Its triangular serrated teeth were each more than three inches long. If a human being were to blunder into it, the trap would shear the person's leg right off.

"These traps will hold anything," Shakespeare boasted. "I'll hear it howling and come on the run. One shot through the brainpan, and that will be that."

"*We* will come on the run, you mean," Blue Water Woman amended.

Shakespeare stared at her a moment. "One of these days your courage will be the death of you, woman."

"As will yours." Blue Water Woman meant it as an innocent remark, but he averted his face and resumed digging with hard, rough motions. She opened her mouth to say he was being childish, then closed it again. Men were extremely sensitive about matters involving their manhood. For all his gray hairs and the decades of wisdom he had accumulated, Shakespeare was no exception.

Blue Water Woman contemplated asking him to go to her

village for help, but she refrained. He would likely construe it as a veiled slight and become madder. So she changed the subject. "I wonder if Zach and Louisa are back yet." Zach King was the son of Nate and Winona King; Louisa was Zach's betrothed. Over a month before they had gone off to distant St. Louis so Louisa could introduce Zach to her kin.

"I hope not," Shakespeare said, not interrupting his digging. "The creature could be terrorizing them, too."

Blue Water Woman hadn't thought of that. Zach and Lou lived in a small valley much like their own about midway between their homestead and Nate's. As the raven flew it wasn't all that far, only twelve miles or so.

"Maybe we should check on them," Blue Water Woman suggested. The Kings were their best friends, as dear to her as her own relatives. Winona, Nate's Shoshone wife, was like a sister. Blue Water Woman had helped tend Zach when he was an infant and watched him grow from awkward childhood into a handsome, if headstrong, young man.

"A fine notion," Shakespeare conceded, "but since that thing paid us a visit last night, odds are it's still hereabouts. We'll wait a day and give these a chance to work." The hole was wide enough to suit him. Taking one of the traps, Shakespeare positioned it in the center and pounded a thick stake through a large circular link at the end of the anchor chain. Then he placed a foot on each of the springs on either side of the jagged jaws. "Now comes the part that always makes me appreciate having fingers," he remarked.

Blue Water Woman bit her lower lip. One slip, and her husband would lose a hand or part of an arm.

Shakespeare applied his full weight. The springs slowly lowered, and the jaws just as slowly opened. Bending, careful to place his fingers between the steel teeth, he pressed the jaws flat. It took some doing because the springs resisted, but at last he succeeded. He wasn't done, though. Next he adjusted the dog and set the trigger pan so the slightest pressure would cause

19

the trap to snap shut. Sweat beading his wrinkled brow, he tried several times, but the pan wouldn't stay in place.

Blue Water Woman's heart was in her throat. "Take your time."

"Yes, my adorable nag." Shakespeare wiped his palms on his pants and bent down again. As delicately as if he were digging a bullet out of a wound, he aligned the pan so it was suspended a few inches from the base, then quickly jerked his fingers back. The pan didn't wriggle loose.

"You were a lot faster at setting traps when you were younger," Blue Water Woman said to lighten his mood.

"I was a lot faster at *everything* when I was younger" was his rebuttal. "Now it's your turn. I'll start digging the next hole over behind the cabin."

Blue Water Woman's task was to disguise the trap. She selected half a dozen thin, straight limbs approximately as long as her arm, trimmed them with her knife, and laid them across the top of the hole, three from side to side, three from top to bottom. Over the limbs she draped long weeds, grass, and pine needles. When she was done the trap was completely concealed.

Shouldering her Hawken, Blue Water Woman headed for the cabin. She could see Shakespeare digging heartily away, and she waved to him when he glanced up to check on her. Taking a few more steps, she abruptly stopped. A by-now-familiar feeling came over her, the sensation of being spied upon. Pivoting, she scoured the vegetation. For a second she thought she saw it: a great, dark form off amid the pines. But on further examination it proved to be the stump of a tree.

Her husband soon had the second hole dug. Shakespeare went through the same routine setting the huge trap, but took only two tries.

Once more Blue Water Woman concealed the device, then moved on to the third and last spot Shakespeare had selected, northwest of the cabin about twenty yards from where he had found prints that first day.

"Tonight promises to be real interesting," he commented. "We should both take long naps this afternoon so we can stay awake."

"I think it is watching us even as we speak," Blue Water Woman warned him.

"I know. My brain feels like it's being fried in grease." Shakespeare gave a toss of his white mane. "Whoever it is will live to regret the games he's playing."

"You're still convinced it's a person and not an animal?"

"It walks on two legs, doesn't it?" Shakespeare rejoined. "The only other critters that do are bears, but only for short distances." He stabbed the shovel into the earth as if into the creature itself. "It has to be human. Or partly, anyhow."

"How do you explain those roars we heard? And the way the thing shook the walls?" Blue Water Woman couldn't see those sounds issuing from human vocal cords. Or conceive of a person *that* strong.

"Guessing is pointless," Shakespeare said. "As soon as one of my traps chops off one of its legs, we'll know for sure."

They spent the rest of the day in anxious anticipation. Blue Water Woman puttered around the cabin, dusting, mopping, and sewing. Late in the afternoon she slid the rocker over near the west window and cracked the curtains so she could mark the downward arc of the sun.

Blue Water Woman hadn't said anything, but she had grave reservations about the use of traps. If they wounded the creature, there was no telling what it would do. Its attack on the cabin had been formidable; she couldn't begin to conceive of what it would do if it went berserk. She trusted her husband's judgment, though, so she held her tongue as the blazing orb dipped toward the towering spires of the lofty Rockies.

"We should take those naps," Shakespeare suggested. He had spent most of the afternoon double-checking his guns and honing his Green River knife on a whetstone until it was as sharp as a saber. "Since it's getting late, let's take them together."

21

"I will try. But I cannot make any promises." Entering the bedroom, Blue Water Woman turned down the quilt and lay on her back fully clothed. Although she was tired from several nights without enough sleep, she couldn't doze off. She tried doing as Nate King once suggested and counted imaginary antelope, but it was little help. She tossed. She turned. Finally, she gave up and glanced at Carcajou. His eyes were open and he was smirking at her. "Can't you sleep either?"

"I might have been able to if you weren't behaving like you have bedbugs in your clothes."

"Is that a pathetic attempt on your part to trick me into taking them off?" Blue Water Woman laughed. Secretly she was immensely pleased her husband still enjoyed being intimate. Most men his age had long since lost interest.

"Not unless you're partial to running through the woods in the altogether," Shakespeare bantered. "If that thing breaks in, we might have to dive out a window."

"I doubt you would fit," Blue Water Woman said. His midsection wasn't anywhere near as trim as it was when they met.

" 'Thou art a boil, a plague sore, or embossed carbuncle in my corrupted blood,' " Shakespeare quoted, and patted his belly. "All I need to do is suck in my gut."

"You would get stuck anyway, and get eaten." Blue Water Woman was jesting, but it was no laughing matter.

Shakespeare rolled his eyes. " 'She shines not upon fools, lest the reflection should hurt her.' "

Since sleep was out of the question, Blue Water Woman offered to make a pot of coffee and they walked to the stream together to fill their bucket. The sense of apprehension that beset Blue Water Woman earlier was gone. She took it as a sign that the creature had wandered off and mentioned as much.

"Who can say?" Shakespeare responded. "Maybe it's taking a nap of its own, resting up for another night of trying to beat down our door."

"Why must you always dwell on the bad side of things?"

"Less disappointments in life that way," Shakespeare bantered. "You can't jump out of the way of a falling tree if you don't see it falling on you."

In under an hour the sun was perched on the rim of the world. From her window Blue Water Woman watched—and dreaded. Soon the sun would relinquish the heavens to encroaching night and a legion of predators would emerge from their dens and hideaways to prowl the dark for prey. Fang and claw would rule until dawn. Death would be given free rein.

Ordinarily Blue Water Woman didn't give much thought to the change that took place after sunset. She was always safe in her cabin. But this night promised to be different. Her anxiety mounting, she sat in the rocker and waited for a shriek or a thump on the outer wall, just as deer, rabbits, grouse, and the like were waiting for the telltale pad of stealthy paws and the snarl of hungry meat-eaters.

Shakespeare lit two lanterns. He placed one on the pine table, another on their dresser in the bedroom. "We're as ready as we'll ever be," he announced. His Hawken and a spare rifle were propped near the stone fireplace. Three pistols girded his waist, and in addition to the Green River knife he had tucked a tomahawk under his belt.

"Are you sure you have enough weapons?" Blue Water Woman asked.

"Better to be armed to the teeth than maggot bait." Shakespeare brought an extra lantern from a cupboard and deposited it near the rifles. "In case I need to go out in a hurry."

Rising, Blue Water Woman set to work on their supper. Since they hadn't done any hunting the past week, she was out of fresh meat and had to make do. From a peg over the counter she took down a parfleche filled with pemmican and chopped a large quantity into small bits. The pemmican she had made herself. It consisted of jerked buffalo meat that she had pounded to a fine consistency and mixed with fat and chokecherries. A favored food among most plains and mountain tribes, it was

23

easy to store, lasted several years, and, most important, "tasted downright delicious," as Carcajou had commented on more than one occasion.

Blue Water Woman filled a pot with water and spooned in the pemmican. She added two cups of flour and half a cup of sugar. After stirring thoroughly, she placed the pot on the stove and got a fire going.

Shakespeare was at the table, the works of the Bard open in front of him. "Old William S. sure did have a wondrous way with words," he commented when she walked over.

"So you've told me," Blue Water Woman said. She cracked the curtain over the west window and saw the sun had set. Her mouth went dry. Taking a long-handled tin dipper from another peg, she wet her throat with a few sips of water.

"Listen to this," Shakespeare said, and read, " ' 'Tis now the very witching time of night, when churchyards yawn, and hell itself breathes out contagion to this world. Now could I drink hot blood, and do such bitter business as the day would quake to look on.' "

"You had to read that, did you?" Blue Water Woman arched an eyebrow.

Carcajou chuckled. "To put us in the spirit of things." He flipped pages and ran a finger down one until he came to the part he wanted. " 'Give me your pardon, sir. I've done you wrong. But pardon it, as you are a gentleman. This presence knows, and you must needs have heard, how I am punished with sore distraction.' "

Blue Water Woman grinned. "I'm not a 'sir.' "

"Don't I know it." Shakespeare gave her the look he reserved for nights he was feeling frisky and quoted from memory: " 'Speak again, bright angel! For thou art as glorious to this night, being o'er my head, as is a winged messenger of heaven unto the white-upturned wondering eyes of mortals that fall back to gaze on him, when he bestrides the lazy-pacing clouds and sails upon the bosom of the air.' "

24

"Have you been nipping at that flask of yours again?"

Shakespeare cackled. " 'Arise, fair sun, and kill the envious moon, who is already sick and pale with grief, that thou her maid are far more fair than she.' "

"False flatterer." But Blue Water Woman smiled. With a large wooden spoon in hand, she stepped to the stove. "The other day you said I was a nag. Now you claim I am as beautiful as the paintings of those angels in your Bible. Make up your mind. I can't be both."

"Wrong, dear heart," Shakespeare said. "In truth, you are a virtuous gentlewoman, mild and beautiful." He paused. "And by virtue of being female you can't help being a nag. All women are. Born that way, I reckon."

"How fortunate I am to be married to a man who thinks he knows everything." Blue Water Woman dipped the spoon into the pot.

"I know women."

"Oh, do you now?" Blue Water Woman began to stir. Suddenly a faint wavering howl rent the night. Not the howl of a wolf or coyote, but a howl torn from the throat of something else. Something more than beast and less than human. "It's back!"

"But a ways off yet," Shakespeare said. "It's just left its lair and is on its way down. I give it another half an hour yet."

The next thirty minutes were an unending agony of suspense. Blue Water Woman busied herself bringing the stew to a boil, added a sprinkle of seasoning, and set large wooden bowls and spoons on the table. Her appetite was gone, but she went through the motions anyway for her husband's sake.

Shakespeare read the whole while, every now and again quoting a passage aloud. At length he closed the book, sat back, and sighed. "Do you know why I like William S. so much?"

"He's the only person who ever lived wordier than you?"

"Are you claiming I'm gabby?" Shakespeare said in mock indignation. "No, I like him because what he wrote is true. He saw people as they are, not as they'd like to be or pretend to be."

"Most of those plays are about people killing people," Blue Water Woman mentioned. She didn't feel much like talking, but it helped take her mind off the creature in the dark. "What is so special about that?"

"Flatheads don't kill Piegans? Sioux don't kill Shoshones? Pawnees don't kill Cheyenne? And the Blackfeet don't kill everybody they get their hands on?"

"As you whites like to say, you are comparing apples and oranges. Those plays are not real life."

"Ah, but there's the rub," Shakespeare said. "Many are based on real events and are just as—"

A sound outside brought them both to their feet—the unmistakable *snap* of metal jaws clamping together. Then came a roar such as no beast ever mouthed, a roar like thunder, an outburst of agony and rage that echoed off the mountains and rolled out across the plain below the foothills.

"It worked! The trap got it!" Shakespeare hastily lit the wick to the spare lantern, then grabbed the handle and stepped to the door. "I'll finish it off while we have the chance!" As he reached for the latch they heard another roar—much closer to the cabin.

"Don't go out there!" Blue Water Woman shouted, spiked by a new thought. His custom-made traps were sturdy enough to hold a grizzly. Once an animal was caught, there was no getting loose. That left only one possible conclusion. "There must be two of them!"

Shakespeare hesitated.

Then, through the door, came heavy, labored breaths. Something scraped against the wood.

Blue Water Woman dropped the wooden spoon and ran to her rifle. Cocking the hammer, she turned as a hideous growl replaced the breathing.

"I forgot the brace!" Shakespeare cried. The stout oak branch

26

was leaning against the wall, and he hurriedly wedged it against the bar. He leaped back just as the door was battered by a fierce blow. The repaired hinge held, but the entire door vibrated.

Blue Water Woman ran to his side. A second blow landed. A third. When each landed there was a heavy *thunk*, almost as if the creature's claws were tearing into the wood. "What—?" she began.

"Did you hear that!" Shakespeare exclaimed. "It's using our ax! The thing is chopping its way inside!"

# *Chapter Three*

For Shakespeare McNair the past week had been a nightmare of uncertainty and unease.

In all his born days Shakespeare had never encountered a creature quite like whatever it was that ransacked their cabin. It was always nearby, always spying on them. He could *feel* the thing's eyes on him whenever he stepped outdoors. Yet try as he might he couldn't find it, couldn't track it down, which aggravated him no end. Among his peers he was regarded as one of the best trackers alive. His wood lore was second to none.

In all his born days, no animal or man had ever gotten the better of him before. Shakespeare was always able to cope with any and all threats. But in this instance his decades of experience counted for naught. It was as if he were a green kid newly arrived from the States instead of the oldest mountaineer on the continent.

Shakespeare suspected the thing was biding its time, waiting for the right moment to strike. The first time they let down their guard would be their last. To know his wife was in danger and not be able to do anything about it filled him with fury—and fear. He lived in constant dread, and wouldn't let her out of his sight. Like a mother hen protecting a chick, he was always there, always hovering nearby, ready to give his life to save hers.

Twice during the past week Shakespeare glimpsed what might have been their elusive tormentor. Once he peered out a window and saw a large dark shape off among the pines that vanished the second he laid eyes on it and left him wondering if he really had seen it or if maybe his frayed nerves had him imagining things.

The second time was a day ago, when Winona traipsed to the stream for water and he tagged along as always. He was scanning the woods and the neighboring hills and mountains when he spotted something on a slope to the northeast. Something big. Something black. Something that lumbered into the trees before he could get a good look. Black bear or the creature, he couldn't decide.

At night Shakespeare always kept all their rifles loaded and all his pistols handy. He found it impossible to get a good night's sleep. Every little sound awakened him, even the creak of their bed when Winona turned over. He was constantly tired. Every afternoon he had to fight repeated urges to take a nap. He was afraid that if he did, Blue Water Woman might go outside while he was dozing and the creature would jump her.

Shakespeare was always on edge, always jumpy. He realized that unless something were done, he would be next to useless when the creature finally made its move. So he resorted to his custom-made grizzly traps. He wasn't optimistic, though. The creature was too demonically clever to let itself be caught. But placing the traps gave him the illusion he was doing something other than sitting around waiting for the thing to pounce.

Then came the sound of a trap snapping shut. Shakespeare wanted to whoop for joy. The thing wasn't as smart as he thought! Eager to end their ordeal, he'd rushed to the door and been as surprised as his wife when a roar sounded close to their cabin. Belatedly it dawned on him that he had neglected to brace the door with the thick branch he had brought in for that purpose.

Now, having done so, Shakespeare gripped the Hawken in both hands and backed up as the door shook to gigantic blows. Right away he knew the creature was using his ax. He had chopped enough wood in his lifetime to know the distinct sound it made.

Yelling to Blue Water Woman, Shakespeare pressed the rifle's stock to his shoulder. More blows were being delivered with unbelievable force in a slow, methodical fashion, a steady *thunk-thunk-thunk-thunk*, as if the thing knew it had them dead to rights and was in no hurry to finish them off. Yet another swing of the ax resulted in a crack appearing high in the door. Not a wide crack, no more than half an inch or so, but a sign the door wouldn't hold out much longer.

Inexplicably, the attack stopped.

Shakespeare nervously fingered the Hawken's trigger. He was anxious to shoot but not to waste a ball. He wanted to wait until he had a clear shot.

"What is it doing?" Blue Water Woman whispered as the seconds dragged by.

Shakespeare shrugged. "Your guess is as good as mine." A hint of movement at the crack sent a shiver down his spine.

The creature was peering in at them. An eyeball was pressed to the opening, a huge, dark, baleful eye, unlike any bear's or other beast's.

Riveted in horror, Shakespeare stared back. He heard the thing breathe, heard giant lungs wheezing like a bellows.

"Carcajou?" Blue Water Woman said.

Shakespeare tried to speak, but his tongue was stuck to the roof of his mouth. He willed his forefinger to curl around the trigger, but it wouldn't respond. He was mesmerized by that eye, that glittering, unfathomable eye—as if it were sapping his will, rendering him weak. Then the thing blinked, and whatever hold it had over him was broken. "Damn your hide!" he fumed, and fired at the crack.

The dark eye disappeared, but whether Shakespeare's slug was to blame or the creature had jerked away, Shakespeare couldn't say. He listened for the thud of a massive body, hoping against hope the thing was dead, but heard only the escape of the breath he hadn't realized he was holding.

"Did you get it, you think?" Blue Water Woman eagerly asked.

A bloodcurdling howl was her reply. A howl of anger more than agony, a howl punctuated by a series of blows to the door that widened the crack and threatened to buckle the increasingly flimsy barrier.

Shakespeare ran to the table, set down the Hawken, and snatched up his spare rifle. Thumbing back the hammer, he rotated and aimed at the opening. He saw something move, a suggestion of bulk, of hair, and he squeezed off a shot.

It had no effect whatsoever.

The creature continued to chop at the door in a berserker onslaught that no barrier could long withstand. Wood chips flew as the ax bit deep again and again.

"What is it?" Blue Water Woman cried, aghast.

Shakespeare didn't have any idea, and didn't much care. All that mattered was killing it. It could bleed, so it was flesh and blood, and anything flesh and blood could be slain. Somehow, some way, he had to stop it once and for all. Dropping the spare rifle beside the Hawken, he filled both hands with pistols and strode up to the door.

"What do you think you're doing? Don't get too close!"

Shakespeare needed to be close, needed to make sure he didn't miss. The pistols were .55-caliber smoothbores, powerful enough to drop a bear at short range. Slivers pelted his face and chest as the gap continued to widen. He shoved a pistol through the opening and felt the muzzle brush against the creature's body. Without hesitation, he fired.

The roar that was ripped from the thing's throat was the loudest yet, like the crash of thunder at the height of a thunderstorm. Hot, fetid breath fanned Shakespeare's face, and the eye reappeared, glaring malevolently. Shakespeare raised the other flintlock, but the eye was there only an instant.

For long, tense moments, Shakespeare waited for the attack to be renewed. When it wasn't, he slowly raised his face to the hole, now wide enough to stick a fist through, and warily peeked out.

"Be careful!" Blue Water Woman whispered.

"Load my Hawken for me," Shakespeare directed. From what he could tell, the creature had departed, but he wasn't about to venture outside to confirm it without a rifle. Remembering the spare lantern, he grasped the handle and held it to the opening. Light spilled outside. What little he could see of the clearing was empty.

"Maybe we should wait until morning," Blue Water Woman said, her fingers flying as she opened a powder horn.

"We did that last time and it got away," Shakespeare said. "Tonight we're ending this, one way or the other."

"I'm coming with you."

"Fine by me." This time Shakespeare didn't object. He needed someone to cover his back. Not to mention he would rather have her close to protect her if need be. Placing the spent flintlock on the counter, he parted the curtains and surveyed the clearing. If the creature was still out there, it was lying low.

Blue Water Woman fed powder into the Hawken and tamped down a ball and patch. Replacing the ramrod in its housing under the barrel, she brought the rifle over, along with her own. "I am ready when you are, husband."

"Bring another lantern." Shakespeare kicked the branch aside, removed the bar, and slowly opened the door. The top hinge had split in half this time and the door sagged, the lower edge scraping the floor. He poked his head out, verified that the creature wasn't lurking anywhere near, and slid out, his back to the wall. Glancing down, he spied moist splotches leading to the north. Blood—proof positive the creature was wounded. Sidling toward the corner, he saw a circle of wetness. Nearby, its long wooden handle glistening crimson, was his ax.

"You've hurt it!" Blue Water Woman whispered. "Hurt it bad!"

Shakespeare prayed she was right, but he wasn't taking anything for granted. The creature had gone around to the side of their cabin, and he poked his head out before committing himself.

A line of drops slanted toward the trees. Shakespeare edged toward the forest, perspiration dampening his palms. He didn't relish the prospect of confronting the thing in heavy brush, but it had to be done.

Blue Water Woman's hand fell on his arm. "No."

"No?" Shakespeare whispered.

She nodded at the woods. "In there it has the advantage. We have driven it off. That is enough for now."

"Enough for you, maybe, not for me." The last week had been proverbial hell, and Shakespeare wasn't putting up with any more. "It might be lying out there somewhere, too weak to move."

"Or it might be waiting for us," Blue Water Woman said. Holding her lantern high, she studied the vegetation. "What is that expression whites have? Oh, yes. Better safe than sorry."

"What is that expression the Flatheads have?" Shakespeare countered. "Better to take an enemy's scalp than have your own hang from a coup stick?" He beckoned. "Like you said, it's hurt. We can't ask for a better chance."

"It is not hurt enough."

Shakespeare looked at her. "How do you mean?"

"We both heard a trap snap shut. We both heard the creature scream. It should have been caught fast, yet it attacked our cabin. Then you shot at it three times."

"Tell me something I don't know," Shakespeare said irritably.

They were wasting valuable time. "What's your point?"

"My point is that it should be hurt a lot worse than it seems to be. The trap, the three shots—there should be a lot of blood." Blue Water Woman wagged her rifle at the drops. "Much more than there is. So perhaps it is not as hurt as we think. Perhaps this is a trick to lure us in after it."

Indecision racked Shakespeare. She made sense. She always made sense. And now that he thought about it, there really wasn't anywhere near as much blood as there should be.

"Tomorrow we will saddle our horses and follow it to its lair," Blue Water Woman proposed.

Shakespeare had tried that the day after they initially found tracks. But his mare had acted up a storm after they'd gone a short ways, fussing and shying and refusing to go on. "Let's check the trap before we go in. I'm sure it's the one by the stream."

Quiet shrouded the night, the quiet of the tomb, a quiet as unnerving as the creature's roars. In the preternatural silence the gurgling of flowing water seemed unnaturally loud. As did the crack of a twig Shakespeare inadvertently stepped on.

"Look there!" Blue Water Woman said, thrusting the lantern in front of them.

The branches and weeds she had covered the trap with had been torn apart and were scattered willy-nilly. Blood rimmed the near side of the hole, much more blood than at the cabin.

Shakespeare gawked in amazement. The trap wasn't there! It had been wrenched out, anchor chain, stake, and all.

"How strong is this thing?" Blue Water Woman marveled.

Thinking of the fireplace poker, Shakespeare didn't respond. He hadn't told her about it to spare her added anxiety.

Blue Water Woman swung the lantern from side to side. "Over here," she said urgently, stepping to the left. "You will not believe this."

Shakespeare believed it, all right. Both metal jaws were twisted and bent. The heavy-gauge springs had been corkscrewed like strands of putty, and the chain was missing. It took prodigious strength to perform the feat, greater than any bear's, greater than any animal Shakespeare ever heard of. Sinking onto a knee, he ran a fingertip over the bent metal. When he raised his hand, drops of warm blood dripped down his finger.

"We need help, husband," Blue Water Woman said. "We must go see Nate and Winona."

Frowning, Shakespeare straightened. It went against his grain to admit he couldn't handle his own problems. "Let's wait one more day. If we can't track the thing down tomorrow, we'll light a shuck for the Kings."

"I'll hold you to that," Blue Water Woman said.

They headed back, her lantern holding the darkness at bay. Shakespeare scoured the undergrowth for the gleam of bestial eyes, but he was disappointed. He gestured for her to go inside ahead of him. No sooner did he close and bar the door than from the west an ululating scream akin to the cry of a woman in labor wafted across the valley.

The distance was hard to judge, but Shakespeare guessed the thing was a quarter of a mile away, or better. So it truly had gone off. But for how long? he wondered. "Try and get some sleep. I'll stand watch."

"Only if you wake me in the middle of the night to spell you," Blue Water Woman said. "You need rest as much as I do."

Shakespeare walked her to the bedroom and tucked her in. As he stood there gazing affectionately down at his wife's lovely upturned features, he reflected on how devastated he would be if anything ever happened to her. Without Blue Water Woman his life would be empty, a meaningless travesty. She was everything to him. " 'Beauty too rich for use, for earth too dear,' " he quoted. " 'So shows a snowy dove trooping with crows, as yonder lady over her fellows shows.' " He smiled. " 'Did my heart love till now? Forswear it, sight. For I never saw true beauty till this night.' "

"You are such a fibber," Blue Water Woman said. "But I love you anyway."

Shakespeare blew out the lantern and closed the bedroom door partway. Taking a seat at the table, he loaded the pistol he had expended, then sat back with his fingers laced behind his beaver hat. The hole in the door bothered him. If the creature returned, it could spy on him unseen.

From a rack above the washbasin Shakespeare selected a towel. He tucked one end between the top of the door and the jamb and draped it over the opening. Retaking his seat, he read for a while, excerpts from *The Tragedy of Julius Caesar*. He never tired of Antony's masterful speech to the fickle crowd, never ceased to be in awe of the Bard's brilliance. "The evil that men do lives after them. The good is oft interred with their bones," he read aloud.

Shakespeare patted the book, fondly recollecting the fateful day he bought it from a family bound for the Oregon Country. Beaver furs were in fashion at the time, and like many an adventuresome young man he earned his living as a trapper. But he didn't trap year-round. In the dead of winter when the waterways were half froze over and snow was piled twelve feet deep, the majority of trappers holed up in cabins and whiled away the weeks reading and swapping tall tales.

One year, late in the summer, Shakespeare had gone to Fort Hall to stock up on provisions and obtain a few books to tide him through the upcoming cold months. But there weren't any to be had, much to his disappointment.

In a talk with Milton Sublette, Shakespeare learned about a party of emigrants who had passed by a few days earlier. Sublette told him one of the pilgrims owned a rare and expensive volume of the complete works of William Shakespeare. At the time the name meant nothing to him, but Sublette insisted the Bard was held in the highest esteem by cultured folk everywhere. So he'd jumped on his horse and ridden hell-bent for buckskin after the wagons, catching up with them in less than twenty-four hours.

The man who owned the book was a Scotsman en route to Fort Vancouver on the Columbia River. At first he refused to sell on the grounds he'd had the book for years. He did agree to let Shakespeare look at it, and the moment Shakespeare held the heavy tome in his hands and beheld the exquisitely tooled leather cover and ran a hand over the large gold-embossed lettering, he was smitten. He had to have it.

Shakespeare offered the Scotsman twenty dollars, and the man laughed. Forty dollars, and the man remarked that it was worth ten times that. Digging out his poke, Shakespeare counted out all the money he possessed, a grand total of three hundred and twenty-four dollars and sixty cents.

The Scotsman stopped laughing. "I'm more than a wee bit tempted, friend," he said, with a glance at his wife and sprouts, "but my sainted mother gave me that book and it would break her heart to learn I sold it."

"So don't tell her," Shakespeare said.

"I just can't. I'm sorry."

Refusing to concede defeat, Shakespeare brought over his two packhorses and unfolded a gorgeous buffalo robe he had skinned and cured himself. "Ever wrapped yourself in one of these, hos? They keep a gent right toasty."

The Scotsman held it to his cheek. "I've seen robes like those fetch a hundred pounds or more in Edinburgh."

Sensing victory, Shakespeare stripped one of his animals and thrust the reins into the Scotsman's hands. "And one horse, to boot. Do we have a deal?"

"You strike a hard bargain, Yank."

Afterward, Shakespeare sat near the fire, silently mouthing the words and inwardly cursing himself for being a fool. The language was foreign, nothing at all like the other books he had read. All those "forsooths" and "enows" and "prithees" drove him to distraction. But he wasn't about to give up, not after paying the equivalent of a year's wages.

And a strange thing happened.

The more Shakespeare read, the more he understood what he was reading. The more he understood, the more he enjoyed the plays. That winter, halfway through *The Tragedy of Hamlet, Prince of Denmark,* he came to the conclusion that old William S. was the greatest writer who ever lived, and from then on it was the only book he read except for the Bible.

Now, beset by drowsiness, Shakespeare yawned and turned a page. A passage caught his eye. "And things unluckily charge my fantasy: I have no will to wander forth of doors, yet something leads me forth."

His eyelids were leaden. Shakespeare closed the book, folded his arms across it, and lowered his forehead. A few minutes' rest and he would be fine. He thought of Nate King, his best friend in all of Creation, the man who was like a son to him. He thought of Winona, Nate's Shoshone wife, and Evelyn, their little girl, and the terrible fate awaiting them if they fell into the creature's clutches. He thought of Zach, Nate's son—and then he thought of nothing more for the longest while.

Shakespeare sat up with a start. Befuddled by sleep, he glanced around the cabin, striving to recall why he was seated at the table. In a rush everything came back to him, and he rose and tiptoed to the bedroom to check on his wife. Blue Water Woman was curled on her side, angelic in repose.

The lantern had burned low and needed more oil. Shakespeare moved to a cabinet to refill it, pausing when he noticed that the towel he had hung over the hole in the door had fallen to the floor. Changing direction, he picked it up. His gaze happened to fall on the opening the creature had made, and fear spiked through him like a red-hot brand.

A huge darkling eye glared at him from the other side, an eye filled with raw hate. Shakespeare dropped the towel and staggered back, clawing for his pistols. Hardly had he touched them when the door exploded inward, the bar and the branch shattering like dry sticks. A hideous, hairy apparition burst inside. Arms as thick as tree trunks looped around his chest, pinning his own to his sides. Shakespeare fought to break free, but he was a babe in the grip of a behemoth. Fangs glittered. Tapered teeth yawned to bite and tear. They swooped at his throat, and he screamed as they sheared into his unyielding flesh.

Shakespeare sat up with a start. Blinking in confusion, he glanced down at himself and was immensely relieved to discover it had been a nightmare, nothing more. His hands shook slightly as he rose and stepped to the bedroom. Blue Water Woman was on her back, sleeping peacefully, the blanket up to her chin. He opted not to disturb her and turned.

Mild shock registered when Shakespeare saw the towel had fallen to the floor. The hole in the door was no longer covered. His pulse quickening, he walked around the table to hang the towel back up. He couldn't take his gaze off the opening, couldn't shake a terrible premonition that when he got there, the same dark eye would be glaring at him. It was silly, a man his age acting like a frightened ten-year-old, but nonetheless he looped to the left, to the counter, and crept the rest of the way doubled over so he couldn't be seen from outside.

Unfurling, Shakespeare put his eye to the opening. Something moved, and for a harrowing instant he thought it was the creature. But it was only a lowly moth drawn by the light, seeking entry.

Shakespeare covered the hole, then poured himself some cold coffee and sat back down. The three or four hours of sleep had rejuvenated him. He wasn't tired anymore, so he stayed up reading and sipping and pondering the strange random quirks of fate. In all the vastness of the Rocky Mountains, why had the creature chosen to bedevil them? Where had it come from? More to the point, how could they stop it?

# David Thompson

Shakespeare recalled the time a mountaineer by the name of Larsen dug a gigantic pit, embedded long stakes at the bottom, and covered the whole thing with tree limbs, all to catch a marauding silvertip that had been making life miserable for trappers in the Green River region. Larsen neglected to advertise the fact, and another trapper, Ike Harigan, had the misfortune to blunder into it. Harigan's mount was killed outright. Harigan suffered a punctured foot and a badly torn leg, but recovered, sought out Larsen, and shot Larsen in the same foot.

A pit just might work, Shakespeare mused. The notion appealed to him, were it not for the week he'd need to dig it big enough.

Another hour passed. Shakespeare dozed off again, awakening once to a loud sound—his own snoring. After that he slept undisturbed until a hand fell on his shoulder and brought him out of the chair coiled for combat.

"Why didn't you wake me up, husband?" Blue Water Woman asked. "I wanted to take a turn."

Shakespeare rubbed his tired eyes and grinned. Both windows were aglow with morning sunshine. "You needed to rest."

Blue Water Woman was fully dressed, her raven hair brushed. "So did you. Now you will be tired when we ride out."

"Ride out?" Shakespeare assumed she was referring to their trek to the Kings, but he had forgotten her brainstorm.

"Today we go after the creature and end this, one way or the other."

# Chapter Four

Among various aspects of the affair that puzzled Shakespeare McNair was why the creature never went after their horses. Most predators would; mountain lions, grizzlies, wolves, they all craved horse flesh. Hostiles would go after them, too; stealing a horse enhanced a warrior's esteem among his people. Not that Shakespeare was complaining. Horses were hard to come by, and he didn't care to have to replace their mounts and two pack animals.

A corral was attached to the rear of the cabin, but the horses weren't in it. A hundred yards to the south was a grassy meadow where Shakespeare often tethered the animals for days at a stretch so they could graze to their heart's content. That was where they had been the whole time.

Every morning and each evening Shakespeare and Blue Water Woman checked on them, and Shakespeare never found anything to suggest that the creature went anywhere near the meadow. Either the creature never realized the horses were

41

there, or it had no interest. Yet another of its remarkable and inexplicable traits.

So now here Shakespeare was, astride his white mare, heading up into the mountains with his Hawken across his legs. Snowcap, as he called her, was the third white mare he had owned, the granddaughter of the original. Except for a tendency toward skittishness, she was as surefooted and dependable as the others.

Blue Water Woman rode a dun. His wife made it a point to never become attached to animals, because, as she once put it, "why let yourself grow fond of something that will die one day?"

"I'll die one day," Shakespeare had responded.

"So you will," Blue Water Woman said, grinning, "but my horse doesn't share my bed."

Practical, but hardly warmhearted. When Shakespeare was a lot younger, before his beard bloomed, he suffered from a delusion all young men did—namely, that females were the kindest, sweetest, most romantic critters on the planet. Subsequent experience had taught him it was a myth foisted by women to hide the fact that womenfolk, by and large, were much more logical and calculating then they let on. Oh, they liked to pretend, to put on an act to lure men in. But it was never the "real" them.

Some men became downright mad when they learned the truth, but Shakespeare just shrugged and bore it. There were things in life no man could change, and the female constitution was at the top of the list. Attempting to change them was like butting heads with a tree. It got a man nowhere and left him with a whopper of a headache.

Shakespeare's musing came to end when his wife declared, "More blood! We have come a long way from the cabin and still the thing was bleeding. It must be hurt worse than I thought."

"Maybe," Shakespeare said. There were only a few sprinkles, not enough, in his estimation, to suggest a wound of any consequence.

Following the trails wasn't difficult. The creature had been in a hurry when it left, as its long strides demonstrated, and hadn't bothered to hide its tracks. Shakespeare leaned back in the saddle and scoured the slopes above, trying to divine where the thing was headed. It had to hole up somewhere.

Of equal interest was why no one had encountered it sooner. A creature that large, that aggressive and violent, was bound to have attracted notice long ago. Yet Shakespeare never heard tell of anyone running into it.

Another mystery in an abundance of mysteries.

About to wind through a heavily thicketed area, Shakespeare drew rein. "Look at these," he said, and bending down, he plucked several black hairs from a thorny bush. He thought they might be the creature's, but they were hairs from a black bear, and whatever they were after, it certainly wasn't a bruin.

"What if we haven't found it by nightfall?" Blue Water Woman said. "I don't relish the idea of camping out overnight."

"That makes two of us, m'lady," Shakespeare said. "We'll head back down well before dark."

"And tomorrow head for Zach's?"

"My intention exactly," Shakespeare agreed. "If he's not there, we'll go on to his pa's. Nate has tangled with more grizzlies and unusual beasties than any coon alive. He'll know how to deal with this thing, if anyone does."

"What if it follows us there?" Blue Water Woman mentioned. "Winona and Evelyn will be in great peril."

Shakespeare hadn't thought of that. The last thing he wanted was to endanger Nate's family. Maybe he should rethink their plan.

Soon the vegetation thinned, and before them rose a gradual slope, barren except for occasional large boulders. Imprinted in the dirt were the creature's tracks, making a beeline for the crest.

Shakespeare clucked to Snowcap and applied his heels. The mare climbed higher, her ears alertly pricked, her nostrils flaring as she tested the wind. He watched her closely. Like her mother,

43

# David Thompson

and her mother before her, many a time she had warned him of danger well before his own senses registered it.

Midway to the top, Shakespeare reined up a second time. He'd assumed the creature was half a day ahead of them, but a clear pair of tracks hinted differently. They showed where the thing had stopped and turned to survey its back trail, and Shakespeare would swear they weren't more than a couple of hours old. Grasping the Hawken, he held it with the stock against his thigh, ready for swift use. "Keep your eyes skinned, wife," he advised.

A sawtooth switchback led them toward a lush tableland. Shakespeare had been there before on elk hunts. A pristine paradise, it was seldom visited by anyone else. He eyed the dense undergrowth as they ascended. If ever there was a prime spot for an ambush, this was it.

"I have that feeling again, Carcajou," Blue Water Woman said.

Shakespeare had it, too, the feeling they were being watched. The mention of the name by which the Flatheads and some other tribes knew him provoked memories of his early days in the mountains, back when French *voyageurs* down from Canada plied the rivers and byways, decades prior to the arrival of trappers from the States. The *voyageurs* were great roamers and enthusiastic explorers. They shared a great rapport with the Indians, and many took Indian wives.

One such specimen, a husky, laconic *voyageur* who had taken a Flathead wife, was responsible for bestowing Shakespeare's Indian name. It was after a battle with the Piegans. A war party had attacked the Flathead village, and in the ensuing bloodbath Shakespeare had slain half a dozen in brutal hand-to-hand fighting. Impressed by his ferocity, the *voyageur* commented that he fought like a "*Carcajou*," or wolverine. The name stuck, and ever since, on blustery winter nights when the Flatheads were huddled in their lodges keeping warm, the tale of the white man who fought with the savagery of the most fierce of animals was often related.

Shakespeare grinned self-consciously. Those had been grand days, grand times! He had been in the flower of his youth. Old age had seemed as remote as the moon. So it always was with young men and women. They exulted in their vitality, unwilling to admit that one day it would drain away like runoff down a sinkhole, leaving them shriveled and enfeebled.

Life was so damned unfair it wasn't funny.

In a few more yards Shakespeare saw where the creature had halted and looked back again. There was no doubt now the thing wasn't all that far ahead, but try as he might he couldn't spot it.

"Look! Up in the sky!" Blue Water Woman urged.

Shakespeare did, and spied a majestic bald eagle winging high on the currents. He didn't understand why his wife was excited until he realized the eagle was circling above something that had caught its interest. Coincidentally enough, the spot was just above the switchback, at the edge of the tableland.

"Maybe it sees the creature," Blue Water Woman said.

"Could just be a rabbit or squirrel," Shakespeare guessed. He waited for the bird of prey to tuck its wings and dive, but the eagle circled a few more times and then winged rapidly westward.

Judging by the position of the sun, Shakespeare figured it was between ten and eleven. Five or six more hours and they needed to turn back. He rode toward the spot the eagle had circled, but when they got there all they found were trees and weeds. Reining up, Shakespeare shifted in the saddle as his wife came up alongside him. "I wish you stayed home as I wanted," he absently remarked. He had tried his best to talk her out of coming, but it had been a waste of breath.

"This is my idea. It is only fair I come along." Blue Water Woman unhooked a water skin from her Flathead-style saddle and uncorked it. "Care for a sip?"

"Ladies first."

"Ever the gentleman." Grinning, Blue Water Woman tilted

the tip to her mouth and gingerly swallowed so as not to spill any down her dress.

When it was Shakespeare's turn, he gulped greedily, oblivious to the water that splashed on his chin and shirt.

"In the light of day the creature doesn't frighten me nearly as much as at night," Blue Water Woman commented, searching the forest.

"The shadows of things unseen are always scarier than the things we know," Shakespeare said. "As monsters go, we should be thankful this one has the decency to abide by the rules."

"What are you babbling about?"

"For starters, it's always gone by dawn." Shakespeare quoted William S: " 'I have heard the cock, that is the trumpet to the morn, doft with his lofty and shrill-sounding throat awake the god of day, and at his warning, whether in sea or fire, in earth or air, the extravagant and erring spirit hies to his confine.' "

"The thing we are after is flesh and blood," Blue Water Woman said.

"A monster in any form is still a monster," Shakespeare nitpicked. "Your own people believe certain lakes are inhabited by water beasts, don't they? And to appease them, your warriors toss dead ducks and rabbits into the water as sacrifices so they can cross unmolested in their canoes."

"So?"

"So even your lake monsters abide by rules." Shakespeare reined to the right and threaded among thin boles and dappled growth. All morning they had heard birds chirp and the cries of other wildlife, but now the woods were preternaturally still, as the woods around their homestead had been the past week.

"When did you hunt here last?" Blue Water Woman asked.

Shakespeare had to think a bit. "Last spring. Remember? I came up right after the snow melted off to catch the elk before they headed up into the high country for the summer."

"You brought home a fine bull, as I recall."

"Eight hundred pounds or better," Shakespeare said. They had dried and salted most of the meat and still had some stored in the cool confines of their root cellar. Next to buffalo, he liked elk best. A thick, juicy slab smothered in wild onions and seasoned with salt and butter was one of life's prime delights. Of course, neither could hold a candle to painter meat. Mountain men from one end of the Rockies to the other were in universal agreement; mountain lion was the tastiest animal in existence. "Why did you ask?"

"If the creature had been here then, you would have come across sign," Blue Water Woman said.

"You'd think so, wouldn't you?" Shakespeare responded, wondering what she was getting at until he glanced down. More giant prints sprinkled the ground, new as well as old. Some had been made months ago and were barely discernible. Others were as fresh as that morning's dew.

"It has been living up here a good long while, but it has not bothered us until recently. I find that strange."

"Count your blessings," Shakespeare said. "Trouble finds us regularly enough without us pining for more."

Another surprise awaited them around the next knoll. Both their mounts suddenly nickered, and the dun shied and tried to run off, but Blue Water Woman spoke sternly and asserted control.

The cause was a gleaming pile of bones in the center of a small clearing. Shakespeare recognized the remains of a long-dead horse, the flesh stripped by scavengers, the skull on its side with the teeth agape. The bones were old, very old, and it was a wonder they hadn't been reduced to the essence from which they came.

Dead horses were a rarity in the wild. Most perished on battlefields or wound up in supper pots, their parts used for everything from sinew string to hide shields.

Skeletons always intrigued Shakespeare. They were Nature's tombstones. Just as cemetery markers bore the names and dates of the deceased, bones told a similar story: the kind of animal, its sex, its general age, and how it died. Swinging down, he nudged a leg bone with his moccasin and the bone rolled over, exposing the bottom of the hoof. "What have we here?" he said, hunkering, his interest intensified tenfold.

"The horse was shod," Blue Water Woman said.

Shakespeare picked up the leg bone. Since Indians rarely used horseshoes, odds were the owner had been white. The craftsmanship was superior, the metal still in excellent condition. The workmanship suggested it hadn't been forged at any of the forts along the frontier.

"Carcajou, look at this."

Blue Water Woman had also dismounted and was examining an object hidden by high weeds. Shakespeare walked over, thinking maybe she had found the body of the rider, but it was a saddle, just about the fanciest saddle he ever set eyes on. The skirt was inlaid with intricately designed silver. Both stirrups and the bow were nearly solid silver, and a silver rim half an inch wide lined the cantle. In addition, inset into the fork where the apple should be was a red gem the size of a hen's egg. Unless he was mistaken, the rig was European-made. How it wound up in the middle of nowhere was beyond him.

"I have never seen a saddle like this," Blue Water Woman breathed.

Rodents and the like had been at the leather, but the silver was untouched and worth a small fortune. To say nothing of the gem. Drawing his Green River knife, Shakespeare pried with the blade, but the gem was stuck fast. "A ruby, you reckon?"

"Like those we saw at the jewelry exchange in St. Louis?" Blue Water Woman bent lower. "It could be, yes."

Shakespeare inserted his blade into the leather ringing the gem and met with success. Bit by bit the ruby came free. A last slice of the knife, and he handed the precious stone to his wife. "You can't say I never give you anything."

Blue Water Woman held the precious stone up to the sunlight. "See how it sparkles! Do you think we can keep it?"

"Whoever owned it is long since dead," Shakespeare said. "We have as much right to it as anyone else."

"The owner's remains must be nearby," Blue Water Woman said. "Let's search for them."

"Another time. We have more important business." Shakespeare rose and replaced his knife in its beaded sheath.

Blue Water Woman's forehead creased. "Is it possible whoever owned this animal was killed by the creature? Maybe the horse, as well?"

Shakespeare hunkered next to the skeleton. The head and neck were intact and untouched by claw, arrow, or lead. Likewise with the rib cage. The right front leg, however, was bent to one side at an impossible angle. The horse had suffered a severe compound fracture below the knee. He discovered why when he parted the grass and groped the soil. "We can't blame this on the creature. The horse stepped into a rut and snapped its leg."

"Then the rider might have survived."

"Not if he was thrown hard enough," Shakespeare said. At a rendezvous he'd witnessed a collision during a horse race in which a trapper was sent sailing over his mount's neck and smashed face-first into the earth. Everyone had laughed and snickered until it dawned on them that the man wasn't getting back up. He couldn't. His neck had been broken.

Blue Water Woman gazed off into the trees. "When this is over I would like to—" A gasp escaped her, and she took a step back.

Rising, Shakespeare felt his blood curdle. A hundred yards away amid a stand of spruce stood a massive black shape he mistook for a shadow until it moved, until it lurched toward them with an awkward rolling gait. "The creature!" he cried, elevating the Hawken. But in the blink of an eye the thing melted into the greenery.

Blue Water Woman pointed. "There! It's circling us!"

49

The creature was gliding at incredible speed from tree to tree and thicket to thicket. All Shakespeare could see were broken patches of black, not enough of a target to take a bead. "Mount up!" he hollered, and the two of them sidestepped toward their mounts. A hasty retreat was called for, out of the woods and into the open, where they could better hold their own.

The dun had other ideas. As Blue Water Woman grabbed for its reins, the horse snorted and backed away. The breeze was to blame. The dun had caught the creature's fetid scent and wanted out of there. Blue Water Woman leaped, snagging its reins on the fly, and grabbed at the saddle to pull herself up. She would have made it had the dun not chosen that instant to take another bound backward. Upended, Blue Water Woman lost her hold and toppled, her rifle jammed underneath her. Involuntarily, she cried out.

Shakespeare sprang to help. As he hoisted her erect, she grit her teeth in torment and arched her spine. "Can you walk?" he asked. Blue Water Woman shook her head, so he wrapped his left arm around her waist and propelled her toward the dun. He attempted to snag the reins himself, but the animal pranced out of reach. Cursing under his breath, he tried again. This time the dun whirled and ran off, deserting them.

Shakespeare had never shot a horse in anger, but he was sorely tempted to do so now. A whinny from the mare gave him something else to worry about. Pivoting, he saw the creature barreling toward them like a bull buffalo. Body hunched forward, it plowed through every obstacle in its path: briars, bushes, even small trees. In another thirty seconds it would be on top of them. "Damn!" he declared.

Blue Water Woman sagged, her lovely face contorted. Scooping her up, Shakespeare ran to the mare and flung his wife into the saddle. He was sorry to be so rough, sorry to cause her more discomfort, but they had no time to spare. Reaching around, he gripped the horn and vaulted up behind her so he could brace her body with his own.

Shakespeare reined to the right as the woods pealed to a ferocious roar. He glanced over a shoulder and saw the creature twenty yards away, churning through the vegetation like a hairy tornado. Facing front, he rode with all the skill at his command, one arm clamped around Blue Water Woman, his other hand holding the reins and the Hawken both.

The traitorous dun was rushing headlong for the switchback—and home.

Blue Water Woman groaned when the mare abruptly veered to avoid a tree. Placing his lips to her ear, Shakespeare coaxed, "Hold on! Once we're safe I'll stop. It shouldn't be long."

Then again, he could be wrong. Glancing back again, Shakespeare was startled to find the creature in open pursuit, flowing over the ground with unbelievable speed, as fast as the mare, or faster. The feat was all the more astounding in light of the creature's uneven, lurching gait.

"Heeyah!" Shakespeare bawled, applying the reins. The mare was doing the best she could, but she had to bear the weight of two people over some extremely rugged terrain. He let her have her head, then twisted to see if the creature had gained any.

It had.

Thirty feet separated them. Shakespeare saw the thing clearly for the first time, and what he saw only added to the mystery.

Seven feet tall, if not more, the creature was three times as wide as an average man and possessed extraordinarily broad shoulders. At their apex was a pronounced hump, akin to the hump on a grizzly. But the creature moved on two legs, not four, legs as thick as tree trunks and as powerful as the pistons on a steam engine. Legs clad in buckskin, not hair. On its feet were huge moccasins constructed from bear paws, complete with pads and claws.

The black hair Shakespeare had found, the black hair that lent the illusion of the creature being covered with fur, came from a knee-length robe it wore, a robe fashioned by stitching the hides of several black bears together. It was crowned by a loose-fitting hood that effectively hid the thing's face. Or, rather, the *person's* face.

"It's a man!" Shakespeare exclaimed. On one hand, the dis covery was comforting. Human beings weren't invincible. A man could be slain. But on the other hand, it was a man unlike any other, a man endowed with the prodigious strength of Samson and the raw ferocity of a grizzly. A man who could bend fireplace pokers and metal traps in his bare hands. A man more monster than human.

Blue Water Woman straightened and stared past him. She said something in the Flathead tongue, something he didn't quite catch.

"What was that?"

"The hunchback of the heights."

Shakespeare wasn't sure he had heard correctly over the pounding of the mare's hoofs and the hideous snarls of their pursuer. "What did you say?"

Blue Water Woman raised her voice. "The hunchback of—!" She got no further. The mare swerved to go around a boulder, and without warning a tree materialized in front of them. Shakespeare saw a bunch of low limbs directly in their path and reined to the left, but it was too little, too late.

At breakneck speed they slammed into the branches. Blue Water Woman was clipped on the head and knocked against him. Like leaves in a gale they toppled from the saddle, Shakespeare with his arm still around her. The ground rose to greet them and they tumbled wildly, Shakespeare losing his hold as they rolled to a stop. He placed his hands flat to rise, but dizziness assailed him and he collapsed, disoriented and distressingly weak.

"Husband?" Blue Water Woman said softly. She lay on her stomach a few yards off, her long hair over her face. "I hurt."

Gritting his teeth, Shakespeare pushed up onto his hands and knees. The sky and the earth were doing a dance and he couldn't quite make up his mind which way was up and which was down. Digging his toes into the earth, he heaved toward her. In midspring a steely hand clamped onto the back of his neck and viselike fingers dug into his flesh. He was jerked into the air and held there as effortlessly as he might hold a child's rag doll.

An image assaulted his confused senses. A horrible, distorted image of a face that wasn't a face, an image so warped and misshapen it couldn't possibly be real, an obscene nightmare given form and substance.

"God help us!" Shakespeare blurted.

"Husband?" Blue Water Woman repeated.

The hand holding him let go and Shakespeare fell with a jolt. He had to reach his wife, had to protect her, but as he rose a blow to the temple felled him like a poled ox. His vision swam, his gut did flip-flops. "I'm here," he croaked, struggling to stand. Inside him an inky chasm yawned and his consciousness began to fade.

"No!" Shakespeare railed, his voice reaching him as if from a great distance. Dimly, he saw a gigantic black mass tower over his wife, saw the creature bend and drape Blue Water Woman over a broad shoulder.

"Carcajou?"

Shakespeare clawed at the dank earth, desperately seeking the will, the energy, to save her. The chasm inside him widened, engulfing him in emptiness. Fleeting despair brought a whine to his lips. Then he passed out.

# Chapter Five

Shakespeare McNair heard someone groan. He was adrift in inky vastness, an ethereal sea where the only sensation was a cool wind. He tried to concentrate, to think, but couldn't. His mind refused to cooperate. His thoughts were sluggish, disjointed, a mishmash of unconnected images and sounds. He was sure he was having one of those dreams where a person knew they were dreaming but were powerless to stop or wake up.

Again the groan sounded, louder this time. Shakespeare wished he could tell whoever was doing it to stop. It distracted him, breaking his concentration, and he needed to focus to make sense of things.

Then a jaw squawked shrilly, and it was as if a finger had been pulled from a dike enclosing his consciousness. A small blue hole appeared in the ether and through it rushed a riot of colors, blues and whites and greens and browns. The earth and sky re-formed before him. He was shocked to discover he was lying on his side in high grass. For the life of him, he couldn't recollect how he got there.

Yet another groan brought the realization that *he* was the one doing all the groaning. Simultaneously, Shakespeare was flooded with vivid memories of the chase, of the hunchback of the heights, of colliding with the low limbs and of being struck on the head. He remembered seeing the creature take Blue Water Woman, remembered vainly trying to reach her. "No!" he cried, and sat bolt upright.

Shakespeare regretted being so impetuous. Pounding waves of pain splashed inside his skull. Dizzy, nauseous, he squinted against the harsh glare of the late-afternoon sun, dismayed that he had been unconscious for hours.

"Blue Water Woman?" Shakespeare croaked, turning his neck. His head protested in the strongest possible terms, and for a moment he thought he would black out again. But the sickening vertigo faded and he slowly rose up onto his knees to take stock of himself and his situation.

Shakespeare wriggled his fingers and toes and moved his arms, and they were fine. No bones were broken, at least. He had a nasty welt on his temple where the creature had hit him, along with a layer of dried blood from a break in the skin. Licking dry lips to moisten them, he swiveled at the hips.

Other things were missing besides his wife. Shakespeare didn't see his Hawken anywhere. Nor hers, come to think of it. He reached for his pistols, but they were gone as well. The only weapon he had left was his Green River knife, which was hardly sufficient to hold off a prowling grizzly or a hungry mountain lion.

Shakespeare inched to his feet and stood swaying like an infant taking its first steps. Guns or no, he would push on after the creature. He couldn't bear to think of Blue Water Woman in the clutches of that hellish *thing*, couldn't bear to imagine what it might do to her, or had already done. "God, please, no," he prayed.

The tracks were plain enough; the creature had gone off to the northwest. Shakespeare willed his legs to move and shuffled after it, gaining strength with every stride. Fear lent him extra energy, fear for the one he loved.

A constriction formed in Shakespeare's throat and his emotions seethed like boiling stew. The thought of losing Blue Water Woman brought tears to his eyes. She was his life's blood, his anchor, his happiness given form and substance. He needed her as much as he needed lungs to breathe. Without her he would wither and die, his advanced years at last taking their toll.

"Damn you!" Shakespeare raged, clenching his fists at what the creature had done. The thing had deprived him of the one person who mattered most, and if it was the last thing he did he would make the fiend suffer, make it howl in agony and die an agonizing death.

The woods weren't as quiet as they had been. A robin was singing to the north. To the south, ravens cawed. A chipmunk he passed scolded him for daring to intrude on its diminutive domain. Proof the creature was long gone.

Shakespeare placed a hand on the hilt of his knife and kept it there. He never knew when a bear or some other predator might rise up out of ambush, but he wouldn't let that deter him. He would push on for however long it took.

At their cabin Shakespeare had his spare rifle and pistols, but on foot it would take days to get there. Days he could ill afford to lose.

The minutes dragged, becoming an hour, then two. Shakespeare regretted letting his wife talk him into tracking the creature down, regretted not going to Nate King's instead. With Nate's help he could have brought the thing to bay and left her with Winona, where she'd be safe.

Lengthening shadows hurried Shakespeare along. The sun was dipping toward the high peaks. Before long night would descend and he would be forced to stop. He couldn't track in the dark. And it wasn't wise to be abroad armed with just a knife when every meat-eater in the mountains was looking to fill its belly. By rights he should find a safe spot to hole up, but he stubbornly plodded on in the belief every step brought him that much closer to his wife.

Soon brilliant multicolored bands painted the horizon, spectacular hues of red, orange and yellow. They faded into twilight, and Shakespeare moved through darkening gloom, scarcely able to see more than twenty yards in front of him. Then fifteen yards. Then ten. By then a myriad of stars sparkled overheard above.

The yip of a coyote stressed the fact that Shakespeare should find shelter until morning. But where? Shakespeare was halfway across the tableland, amid dense forest. The handiest havens were the nearest trees. He debated whether to climb one and spend the night perched in a high fork, and decided against it. Trees were too damned uncomfortable; catching any sleep would be nigh on impossible. He chose to gather a large pile of downed limbs and stacked them next to the trunk of a fir, then sat with his back to the bole. Scooping out a depression with his fingers, he broke the limbs into small sections and arranged them in a small mound. Around the base he sprinkled kindling.

From his possibles bag Shakespeare took his fire steel and flint. On the third strike a tiny spark caught. Bending, he lightly puffed until the spark became a flame. The limbs ignited, and from then on all he had to do was occasionally add more wood.

Shakespeare deliberately kept the fire small so it was less likely to be spotted from a distance. Hostiles might also be abroad. The flames were high enough, though, to keep most animals at bay. Most, but not all. A good-size silvertip, if it was hungry enough, wouldn't let a few puny flames stop it.

Sagging against the bole, Shakespeare reviewed the day's events and felt his eyes moisten again. He'd always counted on having a few good years left with Blue Water Woman, not on having her snatched out from under his nose by a hideous creature spawned in a madman's nightmare. He wondered what she had meant about the "hunchback of the heights." He thought he knew every Flathead legend there was, but no one had ever mentioned a hunchback before.

Maybe it was something new, Shakespeare mused. Blue Water Woman hadn't made as many visits to her people in recent years. She said it saddened her to go. Most of her childhood friends had long since passed on, and of her immediate family only an uncle and a couple of cousins were still alive. Her mother, her father, her brother, her sisters were all gone. So her visits had become less and less frequent, and the last time she went, she took Winona King, not him. At his request. He'd wanted to go off fishing with Nate.

Shakespeare stiffened at a grunt off in the trees, his hand on the Green River knife. A bear was out there somewhere close, but whether it was a black bear or a griz he couldn't say. If the latter, it would make its presence known soon enough.

Shakespeare wasn't unduly worried. Most predators naturally were shy of humans. Even grizzlies, nine times out of ten, turned tail and shuffled off. That tenth time, though, invariably ended badly for the person the griz was after.

Another grunt sounded, nearer now. Shakespeare drew his knife and added a few more pieces of wood to the fire. The circle of light expanded. And there, at the limit of its glow, blazed a large pair of slanted eyes.

*The eyes of a grizzly.*

Shakespeare felt himself tensing up and willed himself to relax. Animals sensed fear, smelled fear, and if the griz sensed his it would be on him in a heartbeat, ripping and rending. He met its unblinking stare with one of his, matching it tit for tat, as it were, and as he sat there waiting for the grizzly to make up its mind whether it was going to devour him, he recalled an incident from long ago, from the days when trappers roamed the

## Join the Western Book Club
## and GET 4 FREE* BOOKS NOW!
### A $19.96 VALUE!

## Yes! I want to subscribe to the Western Book Club.

Please send me my **4 FREE\* BOOKS**. I have enclosed $2.00 for shipping/handling. Each month I'll receive the four newest Leisure Western selections to preview for 10 days. If I decide to keep them, I will pay the Special Members Only discounted price of just $3.36 each, a total of $13.44, plus $2.00 shipping/handling ($22.30 US in Canada). This is a **SAVINGS OF AT LEAST $6.00** off the bookstore price. There is no minimum number of books I must buy, and I may cancel the program at any time. In any case, the **4 FREE\* BOOKS** are mine to keep.

\*In Canada, add $5.00 shipping/handling per order
for the first shipment. For all future shipments to
Canada, the cost of membership is $22.30 US,
which includes shipping and handling.
(All payments must be made in US dollars.)

**NAME:** _____

**ADDRESS:** _____

**CITY:** _____ **STATE:** _____

**COUNTRY:** _____ **ZIP:** _____

**TELEPHONE:** _____

**E-MAIL:** _____

**SIGNATURE:** _____

If under 1 8, Parent or Guardian must sign. Terms, prices, and conditions subject to change. Subscription subject
to acceptance. Dorchester Publishing reserves the right to reject any order or cancel any subscription.

Rockies by the hundreds and the annual rendezvous was the social event of the year.

A prominent man in the trapping trade and co-organizer of the Rocky Mountain Fur Company, Thomas Fitzpatrick, had failed to show up for the 1832 rendezvous as expected, and search parties had been sent out. Alarm mounted when, from a high bluff, one of the search parties spied a Blackfoot encampment. Training their telescope on it, they were appalled to see a Blackfoot warrior astride Fitzpatrick's well-known horse.

Some of the trappers advocated punishing the Blackfeet, Shakespeare foremost among them. The Blackfeet had killed his first wife, Rainbow Woman, and were responsible for the deaths of more trappers than all the other tribes combined. As plans were being finalized for a night raid, word was received that Fitzpatrick had been found alive but on the verge of collapse, wandering afoot along the bank of the Pierres River.

Shakespeare had been one of the first to greet Fitzpatrick on his arrival and had been stunned at how weak and emaciated his friend had become. A walking skeleton, Fitzpatrick could barely speak. He was placed in a tent under warm blankets and given ample nourishment. Within a week he had recovered enough to sit outside the tent and relate his experiences.

It so happened that Fitzpatrick had become separated from his fur company and ended up in a part of the country he didn't know. Blackfoot country, as it turned out, and as he learned to his utter horror when he blundered onto a village and they spotted him before he could conceal himself. He'd fled, pushing his excellent mount to its limits, but in the end his ignorance of the terrain did him in and he had to abandon his faithful but exhausted horse midway up a steep and treacherous slope. He hid in a cramped hole among some rocks and pulled sticks and leaves in on top of him.

For the rest of that day and most of the next the Blackfeet scoured the mountain for him, frequently passing within yards of his hiding place. Fitzpatrick rightfully feared for his life should they find it, and he stayed in the uncomfortable hole the whole time. Not until the third day, when his thirst became unbearable, did he slip out late at night and sneak down to a stream to slake his need.

Confident he could find his way back, Fitzpatrick struck off across country and came to a river. He tried to cross on a small raft he built of old logs, only to nearly lose his life when the raft was dashed to splinters in rapids. In an act of monumental carelessness he had laid his rifle, ammo pouch, and possibles bag on the raft, and they went to the bottom when it broke apart.

For days Fitzpatrick wandered, subsisting on berries, buds, even weeds. He weakened fast, though, and was about stove in when he stumbled on a cow buffalo recently slain by wolves. Tearing what flesh remained from the glistening bones, he made a fire by rubbing two sticks together and ate until he was fit to burst.

Thereafter, Fitzpatrick's luck failed him. Berries and buds became harder to find. He tried to bean birds and small game with rocks but always missed. His hunger mounted even as his body wasted away. Had his deliverers not found him, it was certain he would have perished in the next day or two.

What interested Shakespeare most about the tale, though, was Fitzpatrick's account of his run-ins with wild beasts and how Fitzpatrick comported himself. Time and again the hapless mountain man encountered grizzlies and wolves. Time and again he stood up to them and stared them down.

In one memorable instance, Fitzpatrick had been seated on a rock and a huge silvertip snuck up within six feet of him. At the last moment he sensed it was there and jumped up. The bear stared awhile, then backed off. Fitzpatrick tried to leave, but the grizzly rushed up behind him, so again Fitzpatrick turned and glared at it. Once more the lord of the mountains backed off. Over and over the macabre theater was repeated, until ultimately the grizzly lost interest and wandered off.

On hearing of the close call, Shakespeare commented to the effect that his friend had been extremely lucky.

"Nonsense," Fitzpatrick responded in his typically know-it-all manner. "Luck had nothing to do with it. The Lord was my salvation."

"How do you figure?" Shakespeare had asked.

"Haven't you read your Bible?" Fitzpatrick said accusingly. "The Lord has given man dominion over the beasts of the land and the birds of the air. They are ours to command, to do with as we see fit."

"Tell that to Weaver," Shakespeare countered, referring to a trapper who had been devoured by a she-bear the year previous.

"I saw the tracks. He was running away and had his back to that griz. If he'd stood his ground, it would never have attacked him."

"You're sure of that, are you?"

"Positive. Animals know we are their masters. They fear the very face of man, and with good reason. Or have you forgotten we were sculpted in God's image? Our countenances reflect the majesty of our Maker."

Coming from most anyone else Shakespeare would have figured they were joshing. Fitzpatrick, though, seldom joked or laughed, and there was no question he firmly believed what he was saying.

The conversation had given Shakespeare a lot of fodder for thought over the intervening years. To put the notion to the test, on a number of occasions he had done as his old friend suggested and tried to stare down a bear or other predator. Sometimes it worked. Sometimes it didn't. He concluded it wasn't the mark of God on his face so much as his threatening stance and stare that intimidated animals into leaving him be.

Now Shakespeare hoped the trick would work once again. Because if the grizzly slowly advancing toward his small fire took it into its enormous head to attack, he had no chance whatsoever of escaping.

The bear grunted, a good sign. So far it was more curious than hungry and was sniffing to catch his scent. Into the circle of firelight swayed its broad head, high shoulders, and pronounced hump. Halting, it pawed the ground a couple of times.

The hump reminded Shakespeare of the creature that abducted Blue Water Woman, and he scowled.

An ominous rumble issued from the silvertip's barrel chest, and it reared up onto its hind legs. Almost nine feet tall, it was a third the height of a tree, a mountain of sinew and fur poised to swoop down like an avalanche.

Shakespeare shot to his feet, his eyes locked on the bear's. It growled, but he held his ground. It raised a paw, but he didn't move. He was calling its bestial bluff, taking a gamble that might end with him being reduced to a mangled pile of gory pulp. It was either that or run like hell, and at his age he couldn't outrun a cub, let alone a grown bear.

The grizzly's snout lowered, its lips pulled back to display rapier rows of razor-sharp teeth, and it took a lumbering halfstep toward him.

Shakespeare bared his own teeth and voiced his best imitation of the bear's growl. He raised his knife so the blade mirrored the firelight and wagged it back and forth. An urge to flee came over him, an urge so strong it was all he could do not to give in, and steeling his nerves, he awaited the outcome.

Seconds became a minute, minutes became eternities. The grizzly never made a sound, never moved a muscle. It just stared, its large eyes boring into Shakespeare with burning intensity. A silent challenge, a test of nerves, with his life hanging in the balance.

Beads of sweat broke out on Shakespeare's brow, face, and palms. Drops trickled into his eyebrows and down the sides of his nose, but he dared not wipe them off, not when it might incite a rush. Then a rivulet of salty perspiration seeped into his left eye, causing the eye to tear and blur. Automatically, he blinked a few times to clear it.

Venting a low snarl, the grizzly bent forward as if about to drop onto all fours and charge.

The sustained suspense was more than Shakespeare could stand. Brandishing the Green River knife overhead, he screeched like a banshee. The grizzly reared again, both giant paws upraised, and Shakespeare braced for the rending impact of its four-inch claws. His ruse had failed. His life was forfeit, and so was that of the woman he adored.

Then the silvertip sank down. Baring its fangs one last time, it wheeled and melted into the veil of night, making no more noise than the breeze. The next grunt it uttered was from fifty yards away, the one after that from twice as far.

Shakespeare slumped against the fir, dumbfounded by his deliverance. His knees were shaking and he had to sit down. A laugh slipped from his lips, then another, and presently he was chortling hysterically, unable to control the mirth.

A rumble from his belly brought Shakespeare down to earth. He was hungry, famished in fact. The parfleche containing his pemmican and jerky had been on the mare, so unless he wanted to starve to death he had to give serious thought to hunting game at first light. A spear would help. Arrows and a bow would be better. Ash was the best wood, but he hadn't seen any ash trees so he would make do.

The flames had fallen lower than he liked, and Shakespeare fed fuel to the fire. Leaning back with his hands behind his head, he gazed up through the boughs overhead at an awe-inspiring celestial spectacle. Under different circumstances he would enjoy it greatly. As it was, he couldn't shake a feeling of gnawing anxiety that ate at him like acid. Was Blue Water Woman still alive? Was she hurt? What was she doing at that very moment? Did she know he was on his way? That he would move heaven and earth to save her?

Sighing, Shakespeare sat up. The wilderness throbbed with sounds: the constant roars of bears, the fierce screams of panthers, the plaintive howls of wolves, the anguished shrieks of animals being rent asunder. Bedlam ruled, survival at its rawest, the basic law of Nature borne to savage fruition.

Shakespeare remembered a well-to-do Englishman who came west years before to explore "a bit of your barbaric land," as Ian Smithers described it. Smithers hired him as a guide and went on a "tour" of the central mountains and the adjoining prairie. Shakespeare had done his best to show the man a good time. They'd visited friendly tribes like the Flatheads, the Shoshones, and the Nez Percé. They had gone on a buffalo hunt. They had climbed Long's Peak. And the Englishman's verdict after all that? "Blimey, but you Yanks are bloody daft. Who in their right mind would call a pack of bleeding heathens friends? And don't get me started on the sodding animals. All that beastly caterwauling at night is enough to give a gentleman indigestion."

Shakespeare had disagreed. To him it was routine. Many a night he had been lulled into dreamland by the feral chorus Smithers so despised. Now he sat listening to the din, unable to sleep even if he wanted. To the south a painter screeched and a doe bleated in terror. To the west wolves were on the hunt, their howls cascading from higher regions where elk were to be found.

Much nearer, to the east, a twig snapped. Shakespeare turned, his hand falling to the knife again. It occurred to him he had been premature. Instead of leaving, the grizzly might have circled around, a favorite tactic of theirs when they wanted to catch prey off guard. Another twig snapped, and he leaped to his feet. Prepared for the worst, he peered around the trunk. Something was coming toward him, something big. He couldn't quite make it out, but its size alone hinted his hunch had been right.

The griz wouldn't be denied a second time.

Glancing overhead, Shakespeare gauged the distance to the lowest limb, shoved the knife into its sheath, and took a few steps back, careful to avoid the fire. Legs coiled, he launched himself upward. His frantic fingers wrapped around the limb, and with a lithe swing he forked it and held on for dear life, teetering precariously.

The animal had stopped.

Shakespeare slowly drew his legs high enough to lock them so he wouldn't fall. He wasn't high enough, though. He needed to climb another six to eight feet to put him out of the grizzly's reach. Stretching, he looped his right arm around the next limb above and started to pull himself up. The *crack* of undergrowth gave him incentive to climb faster, but he had only gone half as far as he needed when the brute reached the bottom of the fir. And whinnied.

"Snowcap!" Shakespeare blurted, nearly falling out of the tree in his excitement. The mare's reins were dangling and she was scratched and nicked, but otherwise she didn't appear much the worse for wear. Giggling to himself, Shakespeare eagerly scrambled back down. In his haste he failed to brace his left foot, and the smooth sole of his moccasin slipped out from under him. He careened off an adjacent branch, and agonizing pangs lanced his rib cage. By flinging both arms out he arrested his fall before worse harm was done, and he sat there a minute collecting his breath.

Shakespeare exercised extreme care the rest of the way down. Awash in gratitude, he hugged Snowcap, and she reciprocated by nuzzling his neck. Her head hung in exhaustion as he examined her from nose to tail. Most of the scratches were of no consequence, but low on her thigh was a furrow as long as his hand and on her rump was a deep gash.

"I have some ointment that will have you fit as a fiddle right quick," Shakespeare said, glad to have someone to talk to. "Give me a moment." He stripped off his saddle and saddle blanket and the two parfleches and set them by the fire. In one was a spare pistol, already loaded. He stroked the smooth butt before tucking it under his belt, and said to himself, "It's not a rifle, but it'll do in a pinch."

Wrapped in soft deerskin was the pemmican they had

brought. Shakespeare's mouth watered as he took a bite. He chewed slowly, savoring the taste. His stomach demanded he wolf it, but that would only make him sick.

The ointment, a concoction of Blue Water Woman's, was in a small jar sealed with wax. Extracted from the leaves and stems of a plant with yellow flowers that had yet to be identified by naturalists, then mixed with raw chopped leaves from wild clematis, the ointment was remarkably effective in curing wounds.

Eating as he worked, Shakespeare rubbed some into Snowcap's deepest cuts, then tied her to the tree and spread out his blanket to turn in. He needed to get an early start to have any hope of overtaking Blue Water Woman's abductor. With his saddle for a pillow and his hands folded over the pistol, he closed his eyes and shut out the raucous sounds. Sleep claimed him almost immediately.

As was his habit, Shakespeare invariably woke up shortly before dawn. He had been doing it for more years than he cared to remember. But on this particular morning, when he most needed to be up at daybreak, he slept so soundly he didn't awaken until half an hour after the sun crested the eastern horizon. Furious at himself, he saddled the mare, threw on the parfleches, and rode out without bothering to eat.

The creature's tracks were still as plain as could be and still bearing to the northwest. Shakespeare hoped the thing had stopped for the night and he would find where it had bedded down, but apparently it had pushed on and by now was many miles ahead. He held to a brisk walk in order not to tire the mare, and by noon he had neared the end of the tableland. Ahead rose craggy heights and stark peaks, a wasteland of barren rock where water was scarce and game was scarcer. He should know. He had crossed through once in the inferno heat of summer and almost perished.

The tracks led straight into it.

"So this is where the critter has its lair?" Shakespeare kneed

Snowcap on. Her hoofs rang hollowly on the stone underfoot, like the beat of a drum announcing their arrival. They entered a winding gorge, the walls so high Shakespeare had to lean back to see the top. "I'm coming for you, monster," he declared. Before the day was over, one or the other of them would be dead.

# Chapter Six

Blue Water Woman slowly returned to the land of the living. Her head hurt and she had a cramp in her side, which she relieved by rolling onto her back. A dank scent tingled her nose, and somewhere water was dripping. She remembered being chased by the hunchback of the heights, remembered crashing into a low limb and being gathered up in iron arms, then nothing else until that moment.

Wary of what she would find, Blue Water Woman opened her eyes and couldn't credit her senses. She was in a cavern, a vast, circular bowl carved out of solid rock. The high walls stretched up to dizzying heights, and through a jagged cleft at the top streamed a broad, shimmering band of sunlight that illuminated her surroundings just enough for her to make out the many boulders and stone spires that littered the cavern floor.

Blue Water Woman looked for her captor, but the hunchback was nowhere to be seen. She sat up, her first thought to find a way out of there before it returned, and was startled by a man's low, resonant voice. He addressed her in a language she had never heard but took to be a European tongue. Thanks to Shakespeare, she was well versed in the geography of the planet and its many people. "Do you speak English?" she asked.

"Yes, indeed I do." The man had a distinct clipped accent. "When I was told you speak it, I thought the news was too good to be true. I wasn't aware your kind were conversant with languages other than their own."

"My kind?" Blue Water Woman said, probing the shadows in an effort to pinpoint where the speaker was.

"Indians. You're the first I've ever met face-to-face. This is quite the occasion for me. I can't express how happy your arrival makes me. What is your name, by the way?"

Blue Water Woman told him, stressing, "I did not come here by choice." Rising, she turned toward the spot the voice came from: a clutch of boulders mired in murky shadow. "Who are you? Where is my husband? Did the hunchback of the heights hurt him?"

"Your husband is fine. Kaliban only brought you."

"Is that his name? Eight or nine winters ago he was seen near our village. He tried to steal a horse, but our dogs caught wind of him and our warriors chased him off with their arrows. He fled high up into the mountains."

"Thus, the hunchback of the heights?" The man laughed softly. "An appropriate enough name, I warrant. He was careless being seen like that. But he so wanted to please her by acquiring a steed."

"Her?"

The man didn't answer for a bit, and when he did he changed the subject. "I apologize, madam, for whatever hardship this has caused you. We were in need of a female companion, and you were closest."

"I am a married woman," Blue Water Woman said flatly to disabuse him of any notions he might have. "I would die before I would let you or anyone else so much as touch me."

"Is that what you think?" The man sounded genuinely hurt.

"Please put your fears to rest. You are not here as a consort for Kaliban or myself. It's for her sake and hers alone."

There it was again, the mention of another woman. Blue Water Woman took a few tentative steps. She had yet to be convinced they didn't mean her harm. "Why do you stay in the dark where I cannot see you?"

"My apologies, but it has been an eternity since last I enjoyed the company of another human being besides my loyal servant and the apple of my eye, as Americans like to say." The man coughed. "I confess to being somewhat intimidated."

"*You* are afraid of *me*?"

"Not in the context of being scared of you, no," the man clarified. "It's just that—" He stopped, and a loud sigh issued from the boulders. "Very well. I can't stave off the inevitable. After all, I'm responsible for you being brought to our sanctuary, aren't I?"

Movement heralded the appearance of an enormous form that seemed to rise up out of the very ground. Blue Water Woman realized one of the boulders wasn't a boulder at all but the hunchback, who lumbered toward her with his peculiar shuffling stride. The bear robe that normally covered his upper body had been pulled back, exposing an enormous slab of muscle grotesquely at odds with itself. The parts of his body were misarranged, one hip higher than the other, one leg much lower, among other deformities. Crude buckskin clothes clung to his powerful frame, and from under them jutted large protrusions, as if the flesh underneath were trying to burst out. Inches below his left knee part of the buckskin was missing, ripped off, and the flesh had been sheared almost to the bone. The bear trap's handiwork, she guessed. Yet the hunchback gave no sign of being in pain.

Blue Water Woman's eyes were drawn to the hunchback's thick, brawny arms, to the man the hunchback carried as delicately as a frail flower. And in truth, the man had an aspect of frailty about him, due, no doubt, to his spindly, limp legs, which flapped like leaves in the wind. A shock of white hair crowned the man's hawkish face, hair whiter even than her husband's. Oval green eyes blazed with inner light, dominating shallow cheeks and a thin chin. His skin was abnormally pale, a white sheen laced with veins. His lips were slits drained of natural color. A faded but immaculate purple velvet coat fit snugly over his slender chest, the silver buttons neatly done, the collar smooth. Clean black pants with red stripes clung to his scarecrow legs. His brown shoes were scuffed but laced.

"This will do, Kaliban," the man said, and the hunchback gently set him down, then stepped back to await further instructions.

"He speaks English?" Blue Water Woman said.

"Alas, no. He has no tongue. But I've taught him some over the years, along with a smattering of other languages." The man wistfully smiled. "Among the royal courts of France, Germany, and England I was highly regarded as a linguist. How the mighty have fallen, eh?" He chuckled flatly.

"Who *are* you?"

The man bowed his chin. "My sincere apologies again, dear lady. My manners have lapsed abominably." He looked up, holding himself proudly. "I am Count Stephen Prospero, formerly of Wallanchia. Once, I owned a glorious castle and fine estate, but for the past fifteen years my domicile has been this wretched hole in the earth." His eyes misted over and his Adam's apple bobbed.

"I don't understand," Blue Water Woman said. "My husband has shown me books of life in Europe. Why would you give up all that to live like a mole in a burrow?"

Count Prospero's visage hardened. "Not by choice, I assure you. I was forced out, forced to flee or be beheaded like some common criminal." Stopping, he gripped the hem of his coat and trembled in extreme distress. "When you hear my tale you will be as outraged as I!"

Kaliban gently put a gnarled hand on Prospero's shoulder,

71

his thick fingers dwarfing it, and the count slowly regained his composure. Grateful, Prospero patted the hulking giant. "Thank you, faithful one. As always, I am in your debt."

A special bond existed between the pair, that much was plain. Blue Water Woman surveyed the cavern and spied a pool of water beyond the boulders. "Why am I here? What do you want of me?"

"Always direct and to the point, eh?" Count Prospero smiled. "An admirable trait. Rest assured all your questions will be answered to your complete satisfaction, but first, let us make ourselves more comfortable." He gestured, and the hunchback bent and gingerly lifted him. "Take me to the parlor, Kaliban." As the giant started to turn, Count Prospero beckoned to Blue Water Woman. "Please. Accompany us. You will not be harmed. You have the word of a nobleman of Wallanchia."

A path through the boulders brought them to an open space bordering the right wall where a living area had been arranged. Bearskin rugs covered a dozen square yards. Several crudely made chairs and a long table occupied the center. Against the wall were rough-hewn pine cabinets, and over by the pool sat a wide double-bed with buffalo-hide covers. Next to it was a smaller table.

Kaliban carefully sat the count in one of the chairs, then backed against the wall.

"I trust you won't find the furnishings too distasteful?" Prospero said. "I've done the best I could given the few tools at my disposal, but carpentry was never a strong suit." He indicated another chair. "Please, my dear, have a seat. Permit me the indulgence of treating you as I once entertained legions of royal guests."

Confused and wary yet intensely curious, Blue Water Woman complied. The skin of a black bear had been stretched over a frame constructed of tree limbs and sinew, and was quite comfortable. She smoothed her buckskin dress over her knees before asking, "How long was I unconscious? All night?"

"The sun rose several hours ago," Count Prospero revealed. "I always make it a point to have Kaliban carry me to an outside ledge so I can watch." He glanced at the hunchback. "Fetch some water for our guest. She must be thirsty."

Blue Water Woman watched the giant shuffle to one of the cabinets and take a tumbler from among a row of glasses. Also lining the shelf were a few china plates and bowls. "You made your own dishes, too?" she quipped, knowing full well he couldn't have.

The count chortled. "Would that I could! But no, those I obtained from emigrants on the Oregon Trail. Or, rather, Miranda did. I've warned her it's not safe, but she refuses to listen." He spread his fingers to denote his helplessness. "What is a father to do?"

The china wasn't the only feminine touch. Now that Blue Water Woman had a moment to give the living area a close scrutiny, she noticed other signs: flowers in a vase, a petite pair of women's shoes by the bed, a necklace and a bracelet lying on the small table. "There are just the three of you?"

"Until now," Prospero said. "I hope you feel flattered. You are the only other person to ever set foot in our humble haven. Out of necessity we've had to shun outsiders, both your kind and whites."

Blue Water Woman brought up the point that concerned her most. "How long do you intend to keep me here?"

The count was deliberately vague. "For a while. I promise we will do all in our power to make your stay enjoyable, and when the right time comes we will release you unhurt."

Kaliban was crossing to the pool. Stooping, he dipped the glass in the water, then came toward her bearing the tumbler in a callused palm. His fingers were as deformed as the rest of him; several were stunted, some permanently hooked like claws, and his left thumb protruded from near his wrist. On reaching her chair, he cordially dipped at the waist and offered the refreshment.

"Thank you." Blue Water Woman saw a large dark eye peer at her from out of the folds of the hood, and she smiled.

"Would you care to see the rest of him?" Count Prospero unexpectedly inquired.

Kaliban whined like a dog that had just been kicked and backed away, pulling the hood tighter around his face.

"Come now," Prospero said. "I command you to show her. She will see anyway, will she not, if she stays with us long enough?"

Inarticulate mews of protest gushed from the hunchback as he crouched and vigorously shook the head the count wanted him to expose.

"If he doesn't want to—" Blue Water Woman began.

"I know what is best for him," Prospero said harshly, then added, "His immense size notwithstanding, Kaliban is a child at heart. He has the mental capacity of a ten-year-old. Were it not for my guidance he would be living like a filthy animal, as he was doing when first we met." Prospero speared a finger at the giant. "Show our guest your face!"

Quietly whimpering, Kaliban shuffled to her chair. His hands took hold of the thick hood, but he hesitated, his whimpers growing in volume.

"Do it!" Count Prospero commanded.

A deft flip, and the deed was done. Blue Water Woman expected his face to be as deformed as the rest of him, but the reality eclipsed her wildest imaginings. The hunchback's head was a gruesome mockery of all that was human, a misshapen, abhorrent abomination that caused her to involuntarily recoil. Moon-shaped, it was pitted with scabs and globules of festering pus. Wisps of straggly hair crowned a leathery bald pate. The right eye was large and round and dark, with no iris, no white. Where the left eye should be hung folds of loose skin, drooping like wet clay, and partially covered by the folds, on the left cheek, was a sightless white orb lacking an eyelid. The nose was broad and flat and covered with warts. Bulbous lips rimmed a mouth that perpetually hung open, dribbling drool. Only the teeth were whole and perfect, but they had tapered tips like the teeth of wolves.

At a loss for words, Blue Water Woman could only gawk.

"You can raise your hood now," Count Prospero told the hunchback. "Our guest has seen enough."

Kaliban glumly reached back, his features downcast in misery, and drew the folds up over his head.

Blue Water Woman couldn't say what prompted her to place her hand on his knobby knee. "I am sorry," she apologized. "You caught me off guard. Please forgive me."

The hunchback's good eye fastened on her in surprise.

"It will not happen again," Blue Water Woman said. She pointed at the wound on his leg. "We did that to you, didn't we, with our trap? For that, too, I am sorry. We thought you meant to kill us."

"A botched job, I'm afraid," Count Prospero said. "I instructed him to bring you here, not to terrorize your husband and you. He was supposed to make quick work of it and get in and out without your husband catching on."

"So you knew about Shakespeare all along? How can that be, if you never leave this cavern?"

"Is that his name? How quaint." Count Prospero grinned. "To answer your question, Kaliban told me about you and your husband. He also informed me that he heard you speak English. That was when I realized you suited my purposes perfectly."

"I thought you said he doesn't have a tongue," Blue Water Woman said suspiciously. If Prospero had lied about that, he might be lying about everything, including his pledge to let her go.

"Kaliban, demonstrate for the lady, if you please," the count instructed his servant.

As before, the hunchback hesitated. Prospero had to tell him again. Reluctantly, sullenly, the giant parted the hood and opened his mouth wide. Instead of a tongue he had a mere stub no wider than Blue Water Woman's little finger. Kaliban wriggled it, a pink worm in a sea of teeth, then withdrew his head into the hood like a turtle retracting into a shell, and stepped back.

"He was born that way," Count Prospero said. "Whoever his mother was must have died in childbirth from the trauma of spawning so wretched an infant."

"What a cruel thing to say," Blue Water Woman commented. She couldn't make up her mind whether she liked the count or not. One moment he was courtly and suave, the next he showed a stunning lack of consideration for others.

"Truth is a merciless mistress, Madam. Kaliban's condition, the loss of my legs, they're enough to give a man second thoughts about the beneficence of our Creator." Count Prospero placed his thin hands on his stick limbs. "I ask you. What sort of God allows an injustice like this to happen?"

"You still haven't told me how Kaliban informed you of my husband and me," Blue Water Woman said. The count's habit of evading her queries smacked of rank deception.

"Why don't I show you instead?" Prospero faced the hunchback and moved his hands and fingers in a fluid series of movements.

Sign language, Blue Water Woman deduced. Not the sign talk she was accustomed to, not the signs used by her tribe and others, but a method every bit as effective, for when the count finished, Kaliban went to a cabinet, rummaged on a lower shelf, and brought her a piece of jerked buffalo meat.

"I thought you might be hungry," Count Prospero said. "It will tide you over until Miranda prepares our next meal." He gestured. "Now watch. Kaliban, tell us what you just did."

The hunchback's hands and fingers moved in a series of symbols. He was slower and less graceful, but there was no denying he had the language committed to memory.

"Marvelous, is it not? Who would ever suspect he was intelligent enough?" Count Prospero beamed, a mentor proud of his student. "My mother was deaf as the result of a childhood accident. All my life we communicated by sign language. So when fate threw Kaliban and me together, I hit on using the same means with him."

"You mentioned a purpose for my being here. What is it?"

"Always a fount of questions," Count Prospero said glibly. "All of them will be answered shortly. Over our meal. I can't tell you the last time I enjoyed scintillating dinner conversation. Just one of the many luxuries my nemesis has deprived me of."

Blue Water Woman was anxious to go find Shakespeare. The last she had seen of him was when they collided with the tree, and she was anxious for his welfare. "Perhaps we can have dinner together another time," she tactfully suggested. "I must go find my husband."

"I told you he was fine," Count Prospero said a trifle testily. "But if it will put you more at ease, later today I'll have Kaliban fetch him here."

Like a dog fetching a bone, Blue Water Woman thought. "That would be most unwise. Shakespeare will shoot him on sight."

"Kaliban can be quite stealthy when he needs to be. I'll have him leave a note where your husband is bound to find it, explaining that you are my guest and offering to bring him to you if he sets down his weapons. Will that suffice?"

The man had an answer for everything. "I would rather you simply let me go," Blue Water Woman said.

"As I have tried to make abundantly clear, that isn't possible. You are just what Miranda needs, and after all the trouble I have gone to, I must insist you exercise patience."

Blue Water Woman resented being treated like a prisoner. She went to rise and demand she be released when a new voice intruded, a melodious, feminine voice that had widely different but interesting effects on her host and the hunchback.

"What is it you think I need now, father?"

Count Prospero went rigid in his chair. His hands clamped

onto the chair arms, and his expression was reminiscent of a child caught doing something it shouldn't.

Kaliban, on the other hand, clasped his thick hands in transparent joy and swiveled toward the newcomer, making puppylike noises deep in his throat.

Out of the shadows ambled a stunningly attractive young woman who couldn't be much over twenty, if that. Golden hair burnished with reddish tints adorned shapely shoulders clothed in a well-worn brown blouse a shade lighter in color than her faded, ankle-length skirt. Her face radiated vitality, her complexion was creamy smooth. She had a bounce in her step, a sunbeam in her smile. In her oval green eyes sparkled a forceful frankness that she brought to bear on the count. "Didn't you hear me, father?" She spied Blue Water Woman and stopped short. "My God. What have you done now?"

Taking advantage of the count's temporarily befuddled state, Blue Water Woman said, "He had me kidnapped. It has something to do with you, I understand."

Scarlet tinged the young woman's cheeks and she stormed toward her sire. "You did *what*? After all the talks we had? After I specifically told you not to?"

"Miranda, please," Count Prospero said. "I only ever have your best interests at heart."

Planting her brown shoes in front of his chair, Miranda placed her hands on her hips. A leather belt girded her narrow waist, supporting a long knife on her right hip. "I'm old enough now to know what is best!" she scolded. "Bringing this woman here against her will isn't it."

"But you were pining for female company," Prospero said meekly. "What else was I to do? The nearest forts and settlements are many days away. And if we kidnapped a white woman we would draw undue attention to ourselves. You know we can't have that."

Miranda wasn't pacified. Facing Blue Water Woman, she offered her hand and they introduced themselves. "Please forgive my father. He thinks he is still in the Old Country and can treat people as if they are pieces on a chessboard."

"Daughter!" Count Prospero exclaimed indignantly. "Really, now. I expect more respect from my own flesh and blood."

"As much respect as you have shown Blue Water Woman?" Miranda countered. "I demand you take her back to wherever you took her from, or so help me, I'll do it myself."

"It was Kaliban who brought her," the count said defensively.

"You accuse our sweet hunchback?" Miranda said, and stepping to the giant, who had crouched down with his knuckles resting on the cavern floor, she playfully ran a hand over the giant's hood. "Did you hear that, lovable one? Now he faults you for carrying out his orders. Next he will blame you for rainy days."

It took Blue Water Woman several seconds to identify the sounds that burst from Kaliban in loud, rolling waves—a mixture of snorts, grunts, and strangled noises that constituted laughter. The hunchback was in hysterics, his whole body quaking. His sidesplitting peals echoed wildly off the cavern walls, coming from all directions at once.

Miranda turned to her father, and only Blue Water Woman saw the hunchback's good eye appear at the edge of the hood. Only she saw the unbridled affection it mirrored—the deep, undeniable love.

"Now, then," Miranda declared. "What will it be? Do you have her taken back, or must I do the honors?"

Count Prospero squirmed, a fish caught on a hook. "You are becoming insufferable. All I do, I do for you." He deflated like a punctured buffalo bladder. "Very well. We shall restore Mrs. McNair to her proper place. But first indulge me. Allow us to make up for my questionable behavior by having a meal in her honor. What do you say? Another few hours and she is all yours."

"The decision should be our guest's, not mine," Miranda said. All eyes swung toward Blue Water Woman, even the good eye of Kaliban. She wanted so much to learn who they were and why they were there, but her heart overruled her head. "I would accept if not for my husband. I must be sure he is all right."

"Easily solved," Count Prospero said. "Kaliban and Miranda will go get him, and all of us can eat together."

"I will go too." Blue Water Woman stood.

Her idea didn't go over well with the count. Frowning, he tapped his chair in staccato anger. "Very well. I suppose I must concede or my daughter will disavow me." He waved at the hunchback. "Go with them! Protect them! Bring the husband, and do it quickly."

Miranda touched Blue Water Woman's elbow and led her toward an opening beyond the pool. When they were out of earshot of the decrepit figure in the chair, the younger woman said softly, "I must apologize again. My father was sincere when he claimed he had my best interests at heart, but he went too far this time."

"No real harm was done," Blue Water Woman said. Or so she hoped. She had yet to see how her husband had fared.

"It's just that we are so isolated, so cut off from civilizing influences. My father fears for me."

Blue Water Woman thought she understood. "You have little to worry about with him to watch over you." She jerked a thumb at Kaliban, who plodded along behind them, his good eye fixed on Miranda. "He could hold off a war party."

"Oh, it's not Indians we're concerned about. It's the government of Wallanchia."

"I've lost your trail."

"My father didn't tell you?" Miranda slowed. "The king has put a price on our heads: We are fugitives, Father and I. Outcasts by decree, not by choice." She stopped, and said forlornly, "I can't tell you how much I hate it."

# *Chapter Seven*

The mare started to limp half an hour after Shakespeare McNair reached the rocky region. He immediately reined up and examined her and was tremendously upset to find another gash on her left rear leg below the hock. He had missed it the night before. The leg wasn't swelling up, which was a good sign, but it was still sore enough to slow Snowcap down.

"Consarn it all!" Shakespeare complained while opening the parfleche that contained the ointment. If he pushed on, the swelling would get worse. She needed rest, needed time to recuperate. So either he tethered her somewhere nearby and continued on foot, or he took her down to the cabin and came back up on another horse. Leaving her didn't appeal to him. She was prime prey for every grizzly, mountain lion, and wolf pack. Roving hostiles would steal her at the drop of a feather. Then there was the lack of grass for grazing. And he hadn't seen a lick of water anywhere. The deciding issue, though, was the day he would waste going down and returning. He would be damned if he would leave his wife in the clutches of her inhuman abductor that much longer.

What it boiled down to was a choice between Blue Water Woman and Snowcap. Done rubbing the ointment into the gash, Shakespeare rose and patted the mare's neck. "I'm awful sorry, girl. My wife comes first. We'll go on, but I won't ride you for a spell, not until you stop limping."

Shakespeare replaced the jar, gripped the reins, and led the mare deeper into the maze of bleak stone. Her plodding hoofbeats rang hollowly, the rhythm broken by her limp. He searched for tracks, but the unyielding surface thwarted him. There simply were none.

By nine in the morning Shakespeare was depressed and frustrated. Pushing his beaver hat back on his head, he surveyed the stark heights above. Nothing moved. There was no trace of life anywhere. Not a bird, not a chipmunk, not so much as an insect.

Shakespeare hiked on, flanked on the left by a thirty-foot rock. Ahead, on the left, an opening about eight feet wide appeared. He paused in front of it, debating whether he should go on through. He suspected it was another dead-end gorge, one of a dozen he had investigated already. Tugging on the reins, he started to move on, then abruptly halted.

A cool puff of air had fanned his cheek.

Shakespeare faced into the opening, mystified. The air bore with it a faint hint of moisture. From a spring, maybe, or a tank of collected rainwater. He entered the gap, which twisted and turned for forty or fifty feet before finally broadening out into a fair-size canyon. "I'll be pickled in vinegar," Shakespeare said under his breath. Grass, weeds, and prickly scrub brush covered the canyon floor, along with occasional trees, pines mostly.

Where there was vegetation there had to be water, and with renewed enthusiasm Shakespeare hurried up the canyon to find the source. He hadn't gone far when he spotted a footprint, clear as day, in the dirt. Its immense size, the humanlike toes that ended in claws, the great width: Only one creature had made it. "The hunchback of the heights!" he breathed.

Elated, Shakespeare drew and cocked his pistol. He had a hunch he had found the hunchback's lair, its own private domain cut off from the rest of the world by miles and miles of inhospitable rock. He saw more tracks, scores of them, some leading in, some headed out. His hope that he would soon be reunited with Blue Water Woman mounted.

A hoofprint brought Shakespeare to a stop. It was as fresh as bread out of the oven, made that very morning. He also spotted human prints. Judging by their size and shape they had been made by a woman, but they weren't moccasin tracks, so they weren't his wife's.

"What the hell?" Bewildered, Shakespeare dipped onto his right knee. Each print bore evidence of a low heel and narrow sole, trademarks of shoes worn by white women. But what in God's name was one doing in the canyon? He had to be mistaken. It must be an Indian woman wearing footwear she obtained in trade from whites. But when he thought about it, that made just as little sense. What would *any* woman be doing there?

Shakespeare moved on and promptly made another perplexing discovery: more hoofprints and footprints, only these were old, very old, made over a period of time stretching back weeks and even months. The hunchback, the horse, and the woman had been coming and going regularly over a long period of time. The only logical conclusion was that the hunchback and the woman shared the canyon, actually lived there together, but that was too ridiculous for words.

Greatly confused, Shakespeare crept on. There were now so many tracks, roving all over the place, that trying to separate them was hopeless. The scrub brush thickened, hemming him in, and he wound along a well-worn trail, growing uneasier with every step, anticipating an attack. He breathed a little easier when the brush thinned and verdant grass spread out ahead, along with a few tall trees, including a small stand of pale aspens with their quivering leaves.

Out of the corner of his left eye Shakespeare registered motion. He spun, sighting down the flintlock, but he didn't shoot. Tied to a fir was a handsome roan, saddled and bridled, contentedly nipping grass.

"Next I'll be seeing leprechauns," Shakespeare declared. The roan looked up as he approached but displayed no alarm. "Whoa there, fella," he said, patting its flank and back. The saddle was old but in good condition. Tied on behind it were a pair of saddlebags bulging with items. He started to open one, then happened to glanced off to his right.

Lying in a patch of grass were his Hawken and his other two pistols, scattered at random where the hunchback, apparently, had dropped them.

Stupefied, Shakespeare blinked a few times. For once luck was with him. He ran over and eagerly snatched up his rifle. Other than a few scuffs on the stock it was in perfect shape. The hammer to one of the pistols, though, had been bent, and would need a gunsmith to repair it. He still had the spare, and three guns were more than enough to deal with the hunchback on equal terms.

Grinning in delight, Shakespeare verified that the Hawken and pistol were loaded, then hastened to the mare and shoved the damaged pistol into his holster. "Now to find my wife."

With two flintlocks securely wedged under his wide leather belt and the Hawken in both hands, Shakespeare left the mare next to the roan and stalked toward the canyon wall. He had noticed another opening, larger than before. From it issued the cool puffs of air that initially piqued his interest. He had to wind through some boulders, and there, big as life twenty feet away, was the entrance to what he took to be a cave.

"Got you!" Shakespeare exclaimed. In the dirt in front of the opening were countless prints, the woman's and the hunchback's both. As cautiously as a fox slinking into a henhouse, he stalked forward. But when he was a few feet shy of the opening a foul odor assailed him. A familiar odor, the sickly sweet smell of rotting flesh. He diverted to the right to see what caused the stench, past a few boulders, reborn fear slashing through him— fear his wife had been slain and dumped on a pile of the hunch-back's victims.

He had it half right.

His eyes widening in horror, Shakespeare covered his nose and mouth with his left hand. He had found a pile, sure enough, strewn three feet high for over a dozen yards. A pile of bones, hundreds and hundreds of bones, bones of every shape and size, bones of deer, bones of elk, bones of buffalo and bear, bones of rabbit, squirrel, and grouse. Bones of every animal that lived in the mountains. All bore teeth marks. All had been gnawed on after the animal had been devoured. It was the accumulation of years, maybe decades. Flies swarmed everywhere, flitting from grisly shred to grisly shred. Deeper in maggots squirmed, wriggling and crawling.

Shakespeare had seen enough. He pivoted to leave, but a circle of bone in the middle of the stack caught his attention. Throughout the stack were scores of skulls: bear skulls, painter skulls, deer skulls, marmot skulls, skulls and more skulls. The one in the middle, though, the one that raised the hackles on his neck, was a human skull, the crown caved in as from a mighty blow. Surveying the stack, he spotted more. Not many, maybe ten, all told, but more than enough to heighten his dread for the woman he cherished.

"Blue Water Woman!" Shakespeare breathed. Wheeling, he stormed toward the cave, resolved to find the hunchback and kill it or go to his own reward. He glanced down and cocked the Hawken. When he looked up again, there it was, the creature, the hunchback of the heights, framed in the entrance. Enormous, imposing, it had its head buried in the folds of a bear-hide hood. "You son of a bitch!" Shakespeare growled, raising his rifle. "What have you done with my wife?"

Fingers as thick as railroad spikes formed into claws and rose toward him, and the hunchback vented a guttural growl.

Shakespeare flung himself back out of reach. Quickly, he sighted down the barrel, fixing a bead dead center on the hood. At that range he couldn't miss. The heavy slug would tear through the hunchback's cranium like a red-hot knife through butter. He grinned as he put his finger to the trigger. "I've got you now!"

*"Nooooo!"*

Out of the shadows darted a beautiful young woman with dazzling reddish-blond hair, her face animated by fear. Not fear for her life—fear for the hunchback's. She threw herself in front of him, directly in the bullet's path, and frantically pinwheeled her hands. "No! Please don't shoot him! Kaliban won't hurt you!"

Shakespeare was too astonished to fire. She had to be the woman whose tracks were all over the place, the woman who shared the canyon with the creature. The fact that she cared for him was incredible enough. The fact that she would risk her life was beyond comprehension. But his astonishment increased astronomically when Blue Water Woman calmly strolled out and came toward him with her arms wide for an embrace.

"Husband! You are all right!"

Shakespeare felt her hug him, felt her bosom against his chest, and inhaled the delicious scent of her raven hair. For once in his life he was at a loss for words. He didn't know what to say or do. The world had stopped making sense. The natural order had been deranged and anything was possible.

The hunchback lowered its huge hands and stood as meekly as a little lamb.

"Cat got your tongue?" Blue Water Woman said, playfully tugging on his beard. "Aren't you as happy to see me as I am to see you?"

"Happy?" Shakespeare dully repeated. Anger galvanized him to life, and he exploded, "What the hell is going on? Who is this woman? Why is that—thing—just standing there like that?" He looked his wife up and down. "Damnation, woman! I thought you were dead, or worse! I've been worried sick! I about got ate by a griz! And the whole time you've been cavorting with Lady Godiva, here, and her pet monster?"

Blue Water Woman glanced at the younger woman. "You must excuse him, Miranda. He gets this way when he's flustered."

"Men," Miranda said, as if that explained everything.

Shakespeare didn't know whether to laugh or shoot someone, so he compromised. "Someone had best start explaining, or I'm liable to throw a fit!"

The young woman walked up and politely took his hand. "How do you do. I'm Miranda Prospero. Countess Prospero, actually. A hereditary title passed on from my mother."

"A countess?" Shakespeare said, and blankly looked around. There just *had* to be leprechauns there somewhere. Or maybe a few elves or fairies.

"Countess Prospero of the royal family of Wallanchia," Miranda elaborated. "It's a small country in the Balkans. A mountainous kingdom, centuries old. Our line stretches back to before the birth of Christ."

"A honest-to-goodness countess?" Shakespeare said, irritated by the grin his wife was giving him. "And I suppose there's a count or some such hereabouts, too?"

"Why, yes, my father," Miranda said in all earnestness. "How did you know? He's inside, as a matter of fact, and looking forward to meeting you. We've invited your wonderful wife and you to partake of a formal meal as our guest. Would you be so gracious as to accept?"

Shakespeare couldn't help himself. He reached up and pinched his right cheek, pinched until it hurt. "Well, I'm not dreaming or drunk," he said, more to himself than to anyone else.

An incredible thing happened. The hunchback began to

laugh. In great, gurgling guffaws and loud braying amplified by the canyon walls, he laughed and rocked on his heels, his huge hood bobbing as his head dipped up and down.

"Kaliban likes you, Mr. McNair," Miranda said.

"Is that why he tried so hard to kill me?" Shakespeare retorted.

Miranda moved to the giant and tenderly grasped his wrist. "If Kaliban had truly tried, you would be truly dead. No, he was under orders from my father and had no real intention of harming either of you."

"Could of fooled me," Shakespeare muttered.

Blue Water Woman smiled. "We were on our way to find you, but you have spared us the trouble. Come. I would very much like to hear what the count has to tell us. I find these people fascinating."

"That's one word for it," Shakespeare griped. He felt as if he had walked in on an undiscovered play by old William S. halfway through the third act and didn't know what the hell was going on.

"Please," Miranda said. "I would so enjoy your company. We never have visitors."

Shakespeare squinted at the hunchback. "I wonder why."

"Behave yourself," Blue Water Woman chided. To the countess, she said, "We gladly accept. I will help you cook if you'll permit me."

Miranda beamed. "Thank you. I would be honored. I will show you our stone stove. But first—" She faced the hunchback. "Kaliban, we need a deer. Skin it first, and bring the meat wrapped in its hide. Will you do that for me?"

The hunchback's hands moved in sign language, but not any sign language Shakespeare knew. "What's he saying?" he asked.

"That he would gladly do anything I want," Miranda said tenderly, rubbing the giant's arm. "He and I have been together for so long, he's like a brother to me."

Shakespeare noticed that his wife gave the hunchback a questioning sort of look and made a mental note to ask her why later. "You're not related, though?"

"Oh, no," Miranda said. "He's a foundling. We don't know who his parents were or where he came from." She tilted her chin toward the other end of the canyon. "Go, gentle colossus. Be back as soon as you can. We will be waiting on you."

Kaliban mewed, then hunched over and departed in a rush, the hump on his wide shoulders rolling up and down with each alternate stride of his off-sized legs. He skirted the horses and soon was lost amid the undergrowth.

"As loyal as can be, that one," Miranda said in praise. "Had we ten more like him, we would not be living as outcasts, strangers in a strange land." Giving her glorious mane of hair a toss, she grinned wryly and said, "But enough of that. Follow me, Mr. McNair, and I will introduce you to my father. The two of you can become better acquainted while Blue Water Woman and I are occupied."

So many questions were on the tip of Shakespeare's tongue, but he bit them off and followed his wife and the young woman down a long tunnel that angled to the left. He thought it would bring them to a cave, but he was wrong by half. It opened into a stupendous cavern. They passed a pool fed by an underground spring, went on around a crude hearth chiseled out of stone, to a living area where a white-haired man glumly sat staring off into inner reaches of his own being.

"Father, I would like you to meet someone," Miranda announced.

Shakespeare liked to flatter himself that he was a keen judge of people. He pegged the girl as a strong-willed innocent, a child of the wilds, not the pampered, civilized sort. The count, however, was the opposite side of the coin; cynicism was stamped into every line in his face, cynicism and calculating shrewdness. "Pleased to meet you," Shakespeare said to be polite.

The women wasted no time going off to start the meal. Shakespeare sat across from Count Stephen Prospero, the Hawken across his lap. The prince's piercing green eyes bored into him as if dissecting him piece by piece.

"You can lean your weapon against the wall if you like, Mr. McNair."

"No, thanks. Your hunchback makes me a mite nervous. He has a habit of attacking me every time I turn around."

"He will never lift a finger against you again," Count Prospero said. "Not if my daughter doesn't want him to."

"It isn't your daughter I'm worried about," Shakespeare bluntly admitted.

The count didn't take offense. "Were you aware of all the facts, you wouldn't think so poorly of me. All that I do, all that I have done, all that I will ever do, I do for the good of my daughter. She is all I have left in this world, my sole link to Wallanchia, the country I love, where I was born and raised. The country I served as best I was able."

"Aren't you forgetting Kaliban?"

Count Prospero snickered. "You think him one of us? Oh, that's rich. I will grant you that some of my countrymen weren't blessed with appealing countenances, but none could rival that pathetic wretch in sheer ungodly ugliness." Prospero shook his head. "No, Kaliban is heathen-spawned, the offspring of one of your lowly red races."

"The hunchback is an Indian?" Shakespeare wouldn't have been more shocked if the count claimed Kaliban was related to the president of the United States.

"Abandoned by his mother and father when he was barely months old," Count Prospero said. "Left in the forest to die. But the spark of life burns brightly in his brutish chest. From what he has told me—I've taught him sign language, in case you were unaware—he remembers little of his childhood other than a never-ending struggle to survive. His earliest memories are of running through the forest after game, of bringing deer down with his hands and teeth."

"He hasn't any clue which tribe he belongs to?"

"None whatsoever. The first time he set eyes on a village, he spied on it for days, marveling at the people and how they lived. He had never seen clothes before, never seen a lodge or a horse or a bow. After a week he screwed up his courage and showed himself to a group of women washing clothes in a river. They screamed, and men came to drive him off." Count Prospero thought it humorous. "It was Kaliban's first lesson in the nature of his fellow man."

Shakespeare experienced a twinge of sympathy for the giant and smothered it. The hunchback didn't deserve any sympathy, not after abducting his wife and nearly killing him. "What did he do then?"

"He yearned to live like the people he had seen. He yearned to be accepted by them. So he stole some clothes and again showed himself to the tribe. Again they chased him off. And it sank in that no matter how he tried, they would always do the same. He was different, somehow." Count Prospero laughed. "It took him years to realize the reason. That to us he is repulsive."

"I don't see where it's anything to poke fun of."

"Oh, come now. We're grown men. I'll warrant you've experienced much of what life has to offer, as have I. Surely you appreciate the irony? Kaliban views us as gods, but in truth we are worse beasts than he." A flinty glint came into the count's eyes. "The vile deeds men do in the name of honor! The delusions we foist on ourselves to excuse the most despicable of acts! The kernel of wickedness that lurks in the depths of each man's soul!"

"Speak for yourself," Shakespeare corrected him.

Count Prospero sneered. "Please, sir. Spare me your sham of virtue. No man is the paragon he pretends to be. Humanity is a blight upon this fair world, a plague of ravenous locusts who devour its substance and its soul."

A window had been opened into the depths of the count's being, and it was like gazing out over a bleak and icy landscape. "I don't share your pessimism," Shakespeare said. "I've met plenty of good, decent folks who would give you the shirt off their back if you needed it bad enough."

Count Prospero snorted. "Fools. Dolts and blockheads. Oafs and ignoramuses. Flotsam caught up in the current of their self-absorbed self-importance. They do good because they believe it will earn them a seat on high after they have been torn from this earthly vale."

"No, they're decent by nature and good at heart. Religion is just added incentive, the topping on the pie."

Shakespeare and the count locked eyes, and after a minute the count grinned and said, "We are at polar extremes, you and I, but I respect your right to be misguided. I have known others like you. My own father was equally naive. He, too, believed in the essential goodness of humanity."

"You hold that against him?"

Prospero's face twitched and his mouth scrunched up as if he had sucked on a lemon. "Not that, per se. We are all entitled to our illusions. But I resent the harvest of his stupidity." He had grown as red as a beet.

"What harvest would that be?"

"Later, perhaps," the count said. Lowering his chin to his chest, he placed a hand to his forehead and groaned.

"Are you in pain?" Shakespeare started to rise.

"Be at ease," Prospero said. "My bitterness has festered over the years like a virulent sore, and at times near overwhelms me with the potency of its toxin." Raising his head, he smiled thinly. "I will take your word for it that you are an honest man, although to be honest, as this world goes, is to be one man picked out of ten thousand."

Shakespeare smiled, and continued the quote. " 'That's very true, my lord.' " The next lines leaped to mind. " 'For if the sun breed maggots in a dead dog, being a god kissing carrion—have you a daughter?' "

Count Prospero slapped a stick leg and cackled lustily. " 'I have, my lord.' "

" 'Let her not walk in the sun,' " Shakespeare quoted on. " 'Conception is a blessing; but as your daughter may conceive—friend, look to it.' "

"You know the bard!" Prospero happily declared.

"As I know every pimple on my body," Shakespeare responded.

"Oh, my." The count clasped his hands to his chest. "You have no idea how much I miss his works, how much I miss plays and books and concerts." Tears brimmed at the corners of his eyes. "The royal balls, the theater, the poetry readings, the life at court. I would give anything except Miranda to be restored to my rightful station and privilege."

"If you want to go back to Wallanchia, my wife and I will be glad to help you and your daughter reach the States," Shakespeare offered. "We'll see you to New Orleans, and you can book passage on a ship from there. As for Kaliban, I don't know—" Shakespeare hushed up. The count was crying, openly crying, tears pouring in a torrent. Not knowing what else to do, Shakespeare stood and placed a hand on the other man's shoulder. "Listen, hoss, I didn't mean to get you all rattled."

Prospero's pale, thin fingers glued themselves to Shakespeare's. "Your humanity, sir, touches me deeply. While I am my father's kindred by flesh, I suspect you are more his kindred in spirit."

Shakespeare took that as a compliment. He was searching for the right thing to say to cheer the count up when footsteps padded on the hard stone floor and Blue Water Woman and Miranda hastened up.

"Father! Father!" the beauty cried. "They have come at last, as you always claimed they would!"

In an instant Count Prospero's tears stopped flowing. Wiping his face with his sleeve, he shifted toward them. "Are you certain, daughter?"

"Kaliban just brought word. He saw them from the ridge.

Soldiers are approaching. Many soldiers. And one bears a banner with the royal crest of Wallanchia."

Shakespeare glanced from the beauty to the scarecrow. "You're acting as if it's the end of the world. They're your countrymen. You should be glad to see them."

Count Prospero had been restored to his frigid self. "You know not what you say, my friend. They are our countrymen, yes, but they are also our executioners."

# Chapter Eight

From a high ledge atop the east side of the canyon Shakespeare McNair could see for miles. Raising a hand over his eyes to shield them against the bright glare of the late-morning sun, he saw a column of riders winding westward across the rock wasteland. They were too far off to tell much about them until Count Prospero handed him a folding telescope taken from a cabinet in the cavern.

"Here. Use this. The man whose vanity is pinned to his chest is Duke Viktor Alonzo. He was my father's superior, and my father's destroyer. Because of him I fled to the ends of the earth. Because of him my daughter and I live like animals."

Kaliban had carried Prospero to the ledge as effortlessly as Shakespeare would carry a leaf and was now hunkered behind the count, his good eye visible, fixed on the long line of glittering soldiers and their high-stepping horses.

Adjusting the eyepiece, Shakespeare spotted the duke—a short, burly man with a close-cropped beard and drooping mustachios, his red uniform decorated with rows of gleaming medals. A metal helmet crowned his head. Boots that had been polished to a sheen were thrust through his steed's stirrups. He rode with his chest puffed out, like a peacock on parade. Twenty-three of the remaining twenty-four riders were similarly dressed. All were armed with sabers and side arms and had rifles in saddle scabbards. The sole exception, a tall young man in a blue uniform and beaked blue cap, trotted beside Duke Alonzo. "Why is the one coon different?" Shakespeare asked.

"Blue is the color of the imperial family," Count Prospero disclosed. "Only the king and his immediate family may wear it."

The young man rode with a fearless air, his handsome face aglow with the vigor of youth, a striking contrast to Duke Alonzo's bitter scowl. "He looks a little young to be a king," Shakespeare observed.

"When I was forced to flee my homeland, King Ferdinand was ruler," Prospero said. "Perhaps the young man is one of Ferdinand's sons, in which case he is a prince of the realm. I don't recognize him, although he is vaguely familiar." The count shrugged. "Then again, for all I know Ferdinand is dead or has been deposed. It's been fifteen years."

Miranda gestured at the telescope. "I would like to see, too."

Shakespeare handed it over, saying, "Kings, princes, dukes, and counts. How do you keep track of who is what?"

"The ranking of royals differs somewhat from country to country, but in Wallanchia it is quite simple," Prospero said. "The king is our ruler, naturally. Under him are his sons, the princes. Next in importance are the dukes, his advisers, each of whom oversees a dukedom granted them by his lordship."

"Where do men like you and your father fit in?"

"Each dukedom has a number of counts, barons, and earls who have titled holdings of their own but are nowhere near as powerful. They answer directly to the duke they serve, who in turn relays their concerns to the king. It's not that hard to understand."

"What I don't understand is why they are after you," Blue Water Woman mentioned. "Or how they knew where to find you."

"I will explain why later," Count Prospero said. "As to how—" He glanced at his daughter, who had her eye molded to the telescope. "Blame a headstrong child who never heeds parental advice."

Miranda was oddly loath to lower the eyeglass. "I admit it. I've put our lives in jeopardy, and I am sorry." She turned to Shakespeare's wife. "As you probably know, the Oregon Trail is a few days' ride north of here. Kaliban took me to see it once when I was a little girl, and I've been back scores of times. I never tire of watching the wagons go by and imagining who the people are and what their lives are like."

"If that were all you did, we wouldn't be in danger," Count Prospero said.

"It's a sore topic with us," Miranda explained. "You see, when we arrived in your country all we possessed were the clothes on our backs. When I outgrew mine, my father had Kaliban make me a garment of deer hide. It was smelly and itched, and I hated it."

The hunchback whined pitiably.

Miranda paid him no heed. "I used to lie on a hill near the Oregon Trail and envy those women with their pretty dresses and gay bonnets. Then one day I decided enough was enough. I took a handful of coins from my father's saddlebags and rode up to a circle of wagons. A lady there was all too glad to part with one of her daughter's old dresses."

Count Prospero took up the account. "But it didn't stop there. Against my wishes, she has gone back many times over the years to buy items she felt we needed. Dishes, tools, more clothes, needles and thread to repair my uniform, flour and other food. I warned her there would be talk. I warned her people would tell stories about her and show off the coins she gave them."

Shakespeare recollected hearing such a story himself, years

before. About a wild girl who appeared out of the night at a wagon train encampment and paid for a bunch of towels or some such with a sterling silver coin. He'd assumed the "wild girl" was a settler's daughter and hadn't attached much importance to the account.

"Wallanchian coinage, all I was able to take with me," Count Prospero said. "Eventually word was bound to reach the Wallanchian delegation in Washington and they were bound to take an interest."

"So you're saying those soldier boys down there are scouring the countryside for you because of a few coins your daughter passed around?" Shakespeare said.

"They were important clues the duke needed to our general location," Prospero responded. "Fifteen years ago his agents chased us across Europe to Paris, where I booked passage on a ship to America. They were on the very next vessel, but we disappeared into the interior before they arrived on these shores. Here we have been ever since." The count gazed at the column. "Now he has come in person, so this time there won't be any mistakes. He won't rest until we are dead."

Blue Water Woman was using the telescope. "These mountains cover a lot of territory. How is it they know right where to look?"

"That, I do not know," Count Prospero said. His fingers flowed in sign language, and Kaliban carefully picked him up. "They are still a long ways off, and the odds of them finding our hidden canyon are slim. Still, I feel it wise to return to the cavern. I'll have the hunchback stand guard at the canyon entrance. They will never get past him."

Shakespeare wasn't so sure. Kaliban was formidable, yes, but so were two dozen of the latest European rifles in the hands of professionals. He watched the giant start down, and after Miranda moved to follow, he snagged his wife's wrist and motioned for her to wait a moment. "What do you make of all this? I'm not hankering to be caught in the middle of a blood feud."

"There is more to it than that," Blue Water Woman said. "We cannot run out on them. They might need our help."

"We don't owe the Prosperos a thing," Shakespeare argued. Not after what the count had put them through. "It's not like they're kin or anything."

"I like Miranda, husband. I will stand by her in this. She cannot be blamed for whatever happened long ago. She was only three at the time." Blue Water Woman's tone brooked no argument.

Shakespeare sighed and took the eyeglass. Once she put her mind to something, changing it was as easy as changing the course of a river. "As usual I'll back your play. Go on down. I'll join you in a bit. I want to keep an eye on the duke's outfit." He trained the telescope on the Wallanchian troopers, muttering, "Where's a Blackfoot war party when you need one?"

The column had halted near a ravine. Duke Viktor Alonzo had uncapped a canteen and offered it to the tall young man in blue. Suddenly he and everyone else glanced toward the ravine as if they had heard something. Shakespeare shifted the eyeglass and spied two riders coming out of it, frontiersmen in buckskin and moccasins. As casually as could be, they trotted up to the duke and commenced holding a palaver.

Shakespeare focused on their faces. One was a skinny weasel whose grizzled chin jutted to a point. The other was a stoop-shouldered barrel-belly in a coonskin hat. "Trent and Culo," Shakespeare said aloud. Shifty, grimy sorts, they once made a living at raising plews but were never much good at it. The other trappers never liked them much. Everyone suspected the pair of swiping beaver from traps they didn't own, but no one could ever prove it. The last Shakespeare had heard, after the fur trade died out Trent and Culo hired themselves out as guides to wagon trains bound for the Oregon Country. "Wagon trains," he said thoughtfully. A coincidence? Or something more sinister?

The column was on the move again, Trent and Culo out in front, scouring for sign.

Shakespeare lowered the eyeglass. They were vermin, but they were savvy vermin. They were good trackers, considerably above average, and had a better-than-average chance of finding the Prosperos' hideaway. He couldn't let that happen. His wife had thrown in with Miranda, and if shots were exchanged she might be caught in the crossfire.

Rotating, Shakespeare hastened after the others. He caught up as they were about to enter the tunnel and explained what he had in mind.

The count's eyebrows arched. "You would do that for us?"

"What if they suspect you of lying?" Miranda asked.

"They have no idea I know you," Shakespeare said. "It can't hurt to try." Time was wasting, so he pecked Blue Water Woman and headed for the horses. "Wish me luck." His wife called his name, and he looked back.

"Don't turn your back on Trent or Culo. I remember them well. They never speak with a straight tongue."

"So I'll give them a taste of their own medicine," Shakespeare said with a chuckle. The truth was, the pair had no scruples, and would as soon slip a blade into him as look at him if they were paid enough. He couldn't let down his guard for an instant.

Snowcap was dozing and not all that pleased at having her nap interrupted. Shakespeare examined her leg, glad to find it wasn't swollen. He walked the mare in a circle a few times and she didn't limp once. "That ointment sure works wonders," he commented, forking leather. He held Snowcap to a walk all the way out the canyon, and bore eastward.

Half a mile later, the column came into view. Shakespeare slumped in the saddle to give the impression he was tuckered out, cradling the Hawken in his left elbow. At a shout from Trent the duke elevated an arm, bringing the soldiers to a halt. The duke and the young man in blue moved up next to the two scouts to wait for him.

Shakespeare plastered a friendly smile on his face. "Aren't you boys a little off the beaten path?" he said by way of greeting, and reined up.

"As I live and breathe!" Trent declared. "Shakespeare McNair! I could say the same about you, old coon. What the hell are you doing in this godforsaken spot, anyhow?"

Duke Victor Alonzo cleared his throat. Up close, he had an arrogant aspect to his swarthy features heightened by a zigzag scar on his left cheek. "This is McNair? The one you told me about?"

Trent swiveled. "Yes, sir. He's the feller whose cabin we visited, your dukeship."

"You were at my place?" Shakespeare said, disturbed by the thought of the two thieves helping themselves to whatever they liked. As was customary, settlers never locked their doors when they were gone—partly because everyone trusted everyone else, and partly because locks were damned expensive.

"We sure were." This from sullen Culo. "We've been hired to track down a blond gal and a giant." He brightened considerably. "We're being paid in gold coins!"

Trent motioned sharply. "Tell the whole world, why don't you, you lunkhead?" To Shakespeare he said, "You haven't seen 'em, by any chance? His dukeship, here, might be willin' to give you a coin or two if you have."

Duke Viktor Alonzo cleared his throat and introduced himself. "I am in your country on official Wallanchian business sanctioned by your government. My king has commanded me to hunt down a traitor to the crown by the name of Count Stephen Prospero. We have reason to believe he and his daughter, Miranda, are somewhere in this general area."

"Reason?" Shakespeare said.

Trent tittered and nodded at his partner. "That would be us, hos. We was guidin' a bunch of greenhorn emigrants to Oregon last year when one night this blond gal and a giant feller showed up. The girl bought a pair of shoes from one of the women, then went ridin' off as pretty as you please."

Culo took up the story. "Darndest thing we ever did see. We had no idea anyone was lookin' for her until one of the duke's boys looked us up at Bent's Fort."

Duke Alonzo interrupted. "A family of emigrants on that same train were from Wallanchia. They recognized the coins and sent word to the Wallanchian embassy, which forwarded the information to our king."

"And you came running?" Shakespeare said.

The duke's dark eyes appraised him with a hint of distaste. "Years ago reports filtered to me of a girl buying items from wagon train members with Wallanchian money, but only recently did I receive the corroboration I needed to justify undertaking an arduous ocean voyage and overland trek." He sniffed loudly. "Enough about us. Explain what you are doing in this area, American."

Shakespeare made a show of scrutinizing Duke Alonzo as the duke had scrutinized him. "That's strange. You sure don't look like my mother."

Alonzo missed the meaning. "What does your mother have to do with anything?"

Trent chortled softly. "He's sayin' his business ain't any of yours, your dukeship. That you ain't got the right to pry into his personal affairs. Only his ma does."

"And his ma is long dead," Culo said, tittering.

Duke Alonzo bristled like an irascible badger. "A lowly provincial like yourself, McNair, presumes to insult *me?* For your impudence, I should give an order to have you staked out and flogged."

Shakespeare shifted the Hawken just enough so the muzzle was fixed on Alonzo's chest. "You do, and it will be the last order you ever give."

Trent and Culo chortled, which incensed Duke Alonzo even more. Alonzo began to turn toward the Wallanchian soldiers but froze when the tall young man in the blue uniform finally interjected a comment.

"That will be quite enough."

The change that came over the duke was remarkable. His anger evaporated like morning dew under a hot sun and his mouth curled in an oily, placating smile. "My humblest apologies, Prince. I meant no offense. It's just that this ruffian told me—"

The younger man held up a hand for silence. "I know what he said, my dear duke. I am not hard of hearing." He was every inch the gallant: handsome, broad-shouldered, with clear blue eyes and a finely chiseled complexion, his peaked cap worn at a rakish slant. A holstered pistol was on his left hip, a saber with a bejeweled hilt on his right. Kneeing his big bay up alongside Snowcap, he extended a gloved hand. "I believe this is the custom in your land, is it not? I am Prince Ariel Ferdinand, eldest son of King Ferdinand, ruler of Wallanchia, and heir apparent to the royal throne. At your service, sir."

Shakespeare took an immediate liking to the youngster, who couldn't be much older than Miranda. "That's quite a fancy title you have there, sprout," he said, shaking. "But you still put your britches on one leg at a time like the rest of us."

Duke Alonzo sputtered and dropped a hand to his flintlock. "No one talks to the prince in so cavalier a fashion. You will show him the courtesy that is his rightful due."

"Viktor, please," Prince Ferdinand said. "The man meant no offense. As I have repeatedly tried to make plain, in this country I do not merit special treatment. In America all men are commoners."

Duke Alonzo scrunched up his mouth as if about to spit. "Nobility isn't a garment we shed when we step beyond Wallanchia's borders. We are noble by birth, noble by right, and should be accorded the treatment we deserve in any land we visit."

Prince Ferdinand tilted his head to regard the afternoon sun.

"I would converse with Mr. McNair awhile. Have the men dismount and stand down."

"We will lose valuable time, your highness," Duke Alonzo protested. "According to our scouts, we're close to our quarry. I urge you to reconsider."

"You're the one who insists I exercise my royal prerogatives," Prince Ferdinand said, dismounting. "So consider it an order, not a request. We will move out again in fifteen minutes." He faced Shakespeare. "That is, if you do not mind."

Smiling, Shakespeare slid to the ground. "It beats getting saddle sores, youngster." The remark earned another barbed glance from the duke, which he ignored. "What is it you'd like to jaw about?"

Prince Ferdinand removed his hat and mopped a sleeve across his forehead. He had lustrous curly hair neatly clipped around the ears. "Trent and Culo tell me you are one of the oldest mountain men alive. You must possess a wealth of information about these mountains."

Duke Alonzo had swung his sorrel toward the column and was bawling orders in his native tongue. In unison, the twenty-three soldiers swung their legs from their horses and alighted, standing stiffly at attention until the duke bawled another command. Six hustled forward to ring the prince, arms at the ready, while the rest were permitted to relax.

Shakespeare wagged a hand at the guards. "Do they watch over you when you're taking a bath, too?"

The young prince clapped a thigh and laughed. "They would, I expect, were I to indulge them. But certain functions should be private." He indicated a flat boulder. "Have a seat. I'm eager to pick your brain."

"What makes you so certain I have one?" Shakespeare didn't much care for how Trent and Culo were hovering within earshot, but he didn't make an issue of it.

"Living here as long as you have, you must have heard of the young woman we seek and the giant who attends her."

A logical assumption, but a wrong one. "I don't associate with emigrants much," Shakespeare said. "For the past ten years or so I've pretty much kept to myself. Except to visit a few close friends and spend time with my wife's people, I rarely get out."

"Trent mentioned your wife is a Flathead."

"He's a regular blabbermouth," Shakespeare said, only half in jest. "She's visiting her tribe at the moment. I'm up here after elk. We need to stock up on meat before the cold weather sets in."

"So you haven't seen the girl or the giant?" Prince Ferdinand said.

Shakespeare hated having to lie, but it was for the best. "Can't say as I have, no." He encompassed the regal peaks to the west with a sweep of his arm. "This is mighty big country. Ever hear of a needle in the haystack? Those two people you're after could be anywhere between here and the Great Salt Lake. You might as well head on back to civilization."

"Three people, in point of fact," Prince Ferdinand said, staring at the ground. "The identity of the giant is a mystery, but the young woman might be Countess Miranda Prospero. Her father, Count Stephen Prospero, fled our homeland in disgrace after being caught pilfering funds intended for the king." The prince looked up and wistfully mentioned, "Miranda was my favorite playmate when I was barely old enough to walk. I missed her sorely when they left."

Shakespeare saw something flicker deep in the depths of the younger man's eyes. "Is that why you came along on this hunting expedition? In the hope of seeing her again?"

"The thought did occur to me," Ferdinand admitted. "That, and my father required it of me."

"And you say her pa stole some money?" Shakespeare wasn't all that fond of the uppity count, but he couldn't accept that Prospero was a crook.

"He diverted tax money to fill his own coffers," Prince Ferdinand clarified. "Or so a charge was levied, and so the evidence confirmed." As he said it, he cast a hard look at Duke Viktor Alonzo.

Playing a hunch, Shakespeare inquired, "Was it the duke, there, who made the claim?"

"Duke Alonzo was Count Prospero's superior at the time, yes," Prince Ferdinand said. "Alonzo became suspicious when the tax revenues from Prospero's province were lower than they should be for three years running. He uncovered incriminating records that implicated the count. Word was sent to the king, who ordered Prospero taken into custody while an investigation was conducted. But somehow Prospero received word that troops were coming for him, and he fled to your country with his three-year old daughter."

"Who would be eighteen along about now, I take it," Shakespeare remarked.

"She is five years younger than I am," Prince Ferdinand said. "I have often wondered what happened to her. Whether she was devoured by wild beasts or fell prey to hostile Indians or suffered some other horrible end." He kicked at the dirt with a polished boot. "Her father should never have forced her to accompany him. He recklessly placed her in extreme danger. I can forgive the embezzling of funds, but never that."

"What will happen to them if you find them?"

"Count Prospero is to be escorted back to Wallanchia to stand formal trial. His daughter will become my father's ward and reside at court with us."

Shakespeare remembered what Count Prospero had told him. "You're not going to shoot them on the spot?"

"Heavens, no," Prince Ferdinand said, replacing his cap. "What do you take us for? In Wallanchia the rule of law prevails. We are a monarchy, but an enlightened monarchy. No man can be brought to trial without due cause, and all sentences are subject to appeal to the king, who may overturn any he feels isn't just."

"That's convenient," Shakespeare said.

Ferdinand straightened and clasped his hands behind his back. "I will ask you one last time, Mr. McNair. Have you seen Miranda Prospero or her giant companion?"

"Not in the last ten minutes, no," Shakespeare said, grinning, and stepped toward the mare. "If I do, I'll be sure to tell them you're looking for them." He saw the prince nod at the duke, who in turn snapped his fingers at the six soldiers. Suddenly he found himself staring down the muzzles of six rifles. "What the hell is this?" he demanded, halting.

Trent and Culo were guffawing at his expense.

Prince Ferdinand said tiredly, "I am sorry to detain you, Mr. McNair, but you have not been entirely honest with us. Tell him, Viktor."

"Gladly, your highness." Duke Alonzo strutted up, his thumbs hooked in his black leather belt. "You lied to us, American. Not two nights ago, the giant paid your cabin a visit. Not two mornings ago, you and your wife rode out after him."

Shakespeare didn't need to ask how they knew.

Trent was smirking to beat all hollow. "You see, old man, there's a few things we didn't tell you. For instance, last year, the morning after that gal paid our wagon train a visit, Culo went on with the greenhorns while I tracked the pretty miss and her big pard until I lost their sign about ten miles north of here. I got me a real good gander at that giant fella's tracks. And you know what?" When Shakespeare didn't take the bait, he went on. "His tracks were just like a whole mess of tracks we found near your cabin."

Not to be outdone, Culo bragged, "We tracked your missus and you up into the woods east of here, and saw where you had a lick of trouble. One of your horses ran off. And that giant, he carted off your woman."

"Your wife's dun made it to your cabin, by the way," Trent said. "Lathered to a frazzle."

Duke Alonzo poked Shakespeare in the chest. "Your lies have

availed you naught, American. You are hiding something, and we want to know what it is."

"Please, Mr. McNair," Prince Ferdinand said. "I dislike resorting to force, but you leave me no choice."

"Is this what you meant by an enlightened monarchy?" Shakespeare baited him, and was roundly slapped by the duke. He balled his fists to retaliate, but transformed into stone when six rifle hammers clicked.

"Suit yourself," Duke Alonzo said, relieving Shakespeare of the Hawken and both pistols. "You are coming with us whether you want to or not."

"And any bloodshed that results will be on your shoulders," Prince Ferdinand added.

# Chapter Nine

Blue Water Woman and Miranda Prospero were seated on the lip of the pool in the cavern. Miranda was staring at her reflection and idly swirling the tip of a slender finger in the water. Neither had said much since they returned from the ledge. Blue Water Woman figured her newfound friend was too worried about what would happen should the Wallanchian soldiers find her and her father to be in a talkative mood. For her part, Blue Water Woman was concerned for Carcajou. Shakespeare had a glib tongue and could talk rings around most people, but his plan to persuade the Wallanchians to call off the hunt, or, failing that, to divert them to a different area, was a tall order.

"I'm sorry about our meal," Miranda softly remarked. "We'll have to postpone it until this whole business is over."

"I can wait," Blue Water Woman said, but the young woman did not seem to hear.

"We couldn't even if we wanted to," Miranda went on. "Kaliban never brought us the meat we needed. And now he's keeping watch."

Thinking to ease the young woman's spirits, Blue Water Woman changed the subject. "You like him a lot, don't you?"

Miranda stopped swirling the water, and brightened. "Kaliban? I know some would say he is hideous, but to me he has a heart as gentle as a lamb's. We could never have survived without him. He's been with us since the year we arrived."

"That long?"

"He found us the day after a mountain lion jumped us. My father was saddling up one morning when it sprang on our pack horse. One blow of its paw and it broke her neck. Then it crouched and snarled at us." Miranda shuddered at the childhood recollection. "My father couldn't get to his guns, so he grabbed me and jumped on his horse and we took off out of there as if the forest were on fire. We went about a mile, when his horse stepped into a rut and went down. We were both thrown hard. I was unhurt, but the horse rolled over my father, crushing both his legs."

Blue Water Woman thought of the skeleton and the saddle, and the gem she had dropped when the low limb knocked her off Snowcap. "It must have been a terrible experience for someone your age."

Miranda nodded. "I was so scared. So very scared. I couldn't move my father. We had no weapons. The horse couldn't get back up and just lay there whinnying. We were there a whole day. Then the mountain lion showed up."

"The same one that killed your packhorse?"

"I think so. I saw it slinking toward us early in the evening, its tail twitching, and I screamed for my father to do something, but he was weak from loss of blood and fever and couldn't lift a finger." Miranda shuddered again. "I thought I was done for. I honestly and truly did. The cat couldn't have been more than ten feet away when something flew out of the brush and pounced on it. Kaliban had been passing by and heard my screams. He lifted the mountain lion over his head as if it weighed no more than a blade of grass, then cracked the cat's spine over his knee."

"Were you afraid of him?"

"Not then, not ever." Miranda grinned. "Back then he didn't wear a bear hide, only buckskins. Yet I was so grateful for what he did, I ran up and hugged him. I think it shocked him." She giggled girlishly. "I was the first human being who wasn't scared of him. Thank God I was only three. If I had been older, I might have done like everyone else."

"He is very loyal to you," Blue Water Woman mentioned.

"Just like a brother, yes," Miranda said.

Blue Water Woman suspected there might be more to it than that, but she refrained from saying so. "Was it he who brought you and your father here?"

"Yes. Kaliban carried my father and me, both, and tended my father until he was well enough to sit up and feed himself. It was father who later suggested Kaliban wear a hooded robe." Miranda lowered her voice as if confiding a secret. "My father never could get used to Kaliban's face." She sighed. "My poor, sweet Kaliban."

"Your father did a fine thing teaching him sign talk," Blue Water Woman commented.

"More out of necessity than anything else," Miranda said. "Father had been frustrated because we couldn't communicate with him. Out of desperation he tried sign language. Once we realized how smart Kaliban truly is, we taught him to understand English and Wallanchian and some French." Her gaze roamed over the cavern. "It helped while away the hours. All those long months and years."

Blue Water Woman had been wondering about something. "Why is it you use English more than you use your own tongue?"

"Again, that was father's doing. He's quite the linguist, so I could speak English quite well by the time I was six. He had me use it all the time." Miranda mimicked her father's tone and inflection. "You are in America now, daughter, and you must talk as Americans do. One day you must go out among them, mingle with them, be one of them, and I want you to be ready." Miranda pursed her lips. "Fifteen years, and we're still here," she concluded regretfully.

"When this is over, why not bring your father and Kaliban to our cabin for a visit?" Blue Water Woman proposed. "We would love to have you as our guests for a while." She included the count since she doubted Miranda would come without him.

Miranda's teeth flashed white. "Oh, I would love that! We never go anywhere, never visit anyone." She leaned forward. "Now and then I like to sneak off and spy on neighboring Indian villages. Kaliban always guides me. He has a real knack for finding them." She paused. "I'll lie off in the bushes and watch the people for hours. Especially the women and the girls. I miss the companionship of my own kind." She gave Blue Water Woman's wrist a squeeze. "I can't tell you how much it has meant to me to make your acquaintance."

"It's settled, then. As soon as the soldiers leave."

"The soldiers," Miranda said, and dropped to a whisper. "Did you see the one in blue? Wasn't he handsome? Something about him made me feel I might know him, but how can that be? I was much too young when we fled Wallanchia to remember anyone. The only reason the incident with the mountain lion sticks in my memory, I suspect, is that I was so afraid."

"The man in blue is handsome," Blue Water Woman allowed.

Miranda scooted closer and glanced toward the living area. "Can we talk, woman to woman?"

"Certainly."

"I find myself thinking of men a lot of late. When I visit wagon trains on the Oregon Trail, I catch myself admiring the better-looking ones. Especially those who are about my own age." Miranda blushed as she spoke. "I am becoming a shameless hussy."

Blue Water Woman laughed. "No, you are just like every

other woman. There comes a time in our lives when against our better judgment we are drawn to men like a she-bear is drawn to honey."

"But my father says proper ladies don't do such things. He says ladies don't give rein to their baser passions."

"What does he know? He is a man." Blue Water Woman patted the younger woman's hand. "Trust me. One female to another. The feelings you have, every woman has. The hunger you feel, every woman feels. It is as normal and natural as breathing, and it doesn't make you any less a lady."

Relief and anxiety waged conflict on Miranda's features. "I would like to believe you. But in the back of my mind is a tiny voice—"

"Your father's voice."

"—telling me I must be prim and proper and never make the mistake so many other women make." Miranda morosely folded her arms across her bosom. "It tears me up inside sometimes. There are moments when I just want to scream."

"When that happens, take a few deep breaths and count to ten. Or do what I always did and go for long, quiet walks."

Miranda smiled. "You are very wise. Did you give the same advice to your daughter?"

An old ache filled Blue Water Woman. "I don't have one. I always wanted a big family with eight or nine children, but it was not meant to be. Sometimes life denies us that which we desire most."

"You have a marvelous way with words."

"Credit my husband. Every evening for twenty years he has read to me. The works of Shakespeare. The Bible. And others." Blue Water Woman grinned. "Some of it was bound to rub off."

Their friendly talk was suddenly interrupted by a bellow from across the pool. "Miranda! Mrs. McNair! I need to see both of you this instant!"

"Ever the count at heart," Miranda said, rising. "Always

brusque and demanding. He is my father and I love him dearly, but his attitude leaves a lot to be desired."

"All men have that effect on women," Blue Water Woman joked.

Count Prospero was in his favorite chair, as rigid as a board, wringing his hands in nervous apprehension. "Why hasn't the hunchback reported back yet?" he snapped. "It has been almost an hour. Surely something should have happened by now?"

Miranda squatted and rubbed his arm. "Try not to worry so much. Kaliban will come when there is news to relay."

"My husband is very clever, Count Prospero," Blue Water Woman said. "If anyone can lead the soldiers off the scent, he can."

"You do not know Duke Viktor Alonzo as I do, madam," Prospero curtly responded. "He is evil, that one. Fifteen years ago he murdered my father and tried to have me killed. Now he has traveled to America to finish what his assassins started. He will not let your husband or anyone else stop him."

Blue Water Woman sank into the chair across from his. "The duke murdered your father? Whatever for?"

"Of all the provinces in his dukedom, ours was the finest. We oversaw the best lands. Our tax revenues were higher than anyone else's. Our stables contained over fifty blooded stallions. We owned a grand castle inherited from my grandfather, who had inherited it from his father before him." Prospero's eyes moistened. "I had everything except a loving wife. My wonderful Geraldine died in childbirth, and I have pined for her ever since. She was kindness personified, generous to a fault. Oh, how I miss her."

Blue Water Woman saw Miranda sadden. "You were saying about Duke Alonzo?"

"Oh. Yes. He was always envious of us. His castle wasn't as lavish, his lands weren't as productive. Once he told my father to his face that he thought it immensely unfair for 'a mere count,' to quote his exact words, to be richer than a duke." Prospero grit his teeth. "I tried to warn my father. I told him the duke coveted our holdings and would try to steal them out from under us. But my father refused to heed. He said no one of noble blood could stoop so low. But he was wrong."

Awash in emotion, the count stopped, and Blue Water Woman patiently waited for him to go on.

"One night, about the middle of my daughter's third year, I was in the study reading and heard a commotion coming from my father's chambers. I went to see what it was and stumbled on two hooded rogues who had just smothered my father with his own pillow." Prospero's voice broke, but he resumed moments later. "I shouted for help and rushed toward them, but they were out the window and down a drainpipe in less time than it takes me to tell this. No one else saw them. They left no proof behind. And when the physician examined my father, his verdict was that my father's heart had given out due to old age."

Miranda placed a hand on her father's shoulder. "This is upsetting you. If you would prefer to not discuss it—"

"No, she has a right to know. She and her husband are involved now." Count Prospero took a deep breath. "Not a week after my father's murder, I received word from a trusted friend that Duke Alonzo claimed he had proof I had been skimming tax money, and that word had been sent to King Ferdinand. Agents of the crown were on their way to arrest me."

"What did you do?"

"What could I do?" Prospero rejoined. "I gathered my daughter in my arms, ran to the stable to saddle a horse, and fled. The rest you already know."

"I do not understand," Blue Water Woman said. "Why didn't you go to the king and explain what had happened?"

The count was a while answering, and when he did it was barely above a whisper. "I was afraid. I feared the duke would find a way to have my daughter and me assassinated, just as he did my father. It was foolish of me. I see that now. But I was young and headstrong. Only twenty-five years old."

Blue Water Woman looked at his shock of white hair, his sunken cheeks, his veined, pale skin. "But that would make you forty years old now." She had assumed he was much older.

Count Prospero laughed, a dry rattle rife with bittersweet irony. "Yes, dear woman. I am only forty, but I look as if I am eighty. My hair turned white within six months of arriving here. And thanks to the accident that claimed my legs and my vitality, I am now a shriveled shell, a mere shadow of what I once was."

"Let's not dwell on that, Father," Miranda said.

"I know. You are tired of my carping on the cruel outworking of fickle fate." Her father mustered a wan grin. "But can you blame me? Once, I had it all. Everything a man can desire. And from so lofty an estate I have been reduced to *this*." He flicked a hand down over his withered body. "How the noble have fallen!"

Blue Water Woman mulled his latest revelations. "There is one thing yet that puzzles me. Why, after all these years, has the duke come after you? Surely you aren't a threat to him."

Miranda was the one who answered. "We are no threat at all. My father has no proof Duke Alonzo murdered my grandfather. He has no proof Duke Alonzo trumped up charges against him to strip him of Prospero Province."

"You want to know why?" the count said bitterly. "I'll tell you why! Viktor Alonzo is a devious schemer, as crafty as a fox, as ruthless as a rabid cur. His plot against the Prospero family was foolproof—except I escaped. I am a loose end. And Viktor does not like loose ends. So he has ventured all this way to America to finish what he started all those years ago."

Blue Water Woman disagreed. There had to be more to it than that. The smart thing for the duke to have done was to stay in Wallanchia. So what if reports had spread of a mysterious young woman who visited wagon trains and paid for goods with Wallanchian money? There was no link to him.

"Alonzo will never find us, Father," Miranda declared. "You can rest easy."

"Would that I could," Count Prospero said morosely. "I thought we were safe here. I thought it would take millennia of searching for him to ferret us out. Yet now he's almost at our virtual doorstep, a company of crack troops at his command." Prospero resumed wringing his hands. "The fiend is destined to plague me into the grave."

"Calm yourself," Miranda urged. "So long as breath remains, we must never give up. We are Prosperos, are we not, from an illustrious and proud lineage? Grandfather would shudder in his grave were he to see us cower before a despicable swine like Viktor Alonzo."

"I just wish we knew what was going on," the count lamented.

Almost on cue, from out of the shadows rushed Kaliban, the hood down around his shoulders, his misshapen countenance animated by great urgency. Fingers flying, he relayed a message that set the count to muttering under his breath and Miranda to gasping in consternation. She turned to Blue Water Woman. "He says your husband has been taken prisoner. The soldiers are still traveling in our direction, led by the two men in buckskin your husband mentioned."

Count Prospero clutched his daughter's forearm. "We must flee! We must head farther west, deeper into the wilderness, where Alonzo and his men can never find us!"

"And abandon Mr. McNair?" Miranda said.

"He won't come to any harm," Count Prospero snapped. "It is us Alonzo wants! McNair will be released eventually."

"Perhaps. Perhaps not. We cannot take anything for granted, not where the duke is concerned." Miranda squared her shoulders. "I'll need a rifle. So will Blue Water Woman. She can use one of our extra ammunition pouches and powder horns."

"What are you up to, daughter?" the count demanded.

"Fortune has smiled on the duke so far. He might yet find our sanctuary. When he does, we will be ready for him."

Count Prospero was whiter than ever. "Have you lost your senses, child? The four of us against a company of Wallanchia's

117

finest? They will slay us with ease, and the secret we share, the secret that could cost the duke his head, will be buried with us."

Miranda had removed a yellow ribbon from a pocket in her skirt and was tying her long hair into a ponytail. "We are not as helpless as all that, father. I am a good shot. So is Blue Water Woman, I'd warrant. And Kaliban is an army unto himself. You've said so yourself many times." Miranda winked at him. "We just might give the duke a surprise he will never forget." She dashed off, the hunchback at her side.

"No, you mustn't!" Count Prospero caught hold of Blue Water Woman's hand. "Talk to her! Please! You're older, more mature. You must recognize the futility of defiance. Our only recourse is to run."

"Did running away do you any good the last time" Blue Water Woman said, and pried his fingers loose. "They have my husband. For that reason alone I will stand up to them." Stepping around him, Blue Water Woman moved toward a tall pine cabinet Kaliban had just opened.

Prospero braced himself against the chair and rose as high as his arms allowed. "You'll all be killed!" he cried shrilly.

Miranda accepted a rifle and ammo pouch and slung the pouch across her chest. "We must hurry. It will not take the duke long to reach the canyon entrance."

"Maybe he will ride by without noticing. My husband almost did." Blue Water Woman accepted a Hawken similar to her own and began loading it.

To Kaliban Miranda said, "Go on ahead. Watch for them, but do not let them see you. Under no circumstances are you to attack them. They have many rifles, sweet one, more than even you can withstand. I do not want you hurt."

Blue Water Woman thought of the wound inflicted by the bear trap, and those Shakespeare inflicted when he fired through their shattered door, and remorse pricked her conscience. Had they only known how truly tenderhearted the hunchback was, they would never have taken such drastic measures.

Miranda led the way out the tunnel. As they raced into the sunlight she slowed to say, "If something should happen to Kaliban and me, will you do me a favor?"

"I will do what I can to help your father, yes," Blue Water Woman anticipated the request.

"Take him far away from here, out of that dirty hole we've called our home," Miranda requested. "I've often thought St. Louis would be a nice place to live. Or New Orleans. Somewhere we could lose ourselves in the crowds." She jogged on. "If not for Kaliban, I'd have dragged my father east ages ago. But I won't desert my brother, not after all he has done for us."

The roan was still tied to the tree. Miranda swung up, then leaned down and offered her hand. Riding double, they trotted toward the north end of the canyon. "I am sorry to have embroiled you in our troubles," Miranda said. "I never told my father to have Kaliban fetch you. It was his idea, done behind my back because he knew I would disapprove."

"Water over the falls," Blue Water Woman said. "Now we must concentrate on rescuing my husband." Against two dozen heavily armed troops, that promised to be quite a challenge.

"I have an idea along those lines."

"What kind of idea?" Blue Water Woman inquired, and was mystified when the younger woman didn't say anything—not until a minute later—as they rode along a winding trail through prickly brush.

"This nightmare must end," Miranda flatly stated. "I am so tired, my friend. Tired of the cavern, tired of my father ranting on and on, tired of not being able to mingle with my own kind. Tired of never having nice clothes to wear. Tired of so very much."

Shortly, they neared the canyon entrance. It was Blue Water Woman who spotted the hunchback high on the cliff to the right of the gap, windmilling his huge arms. She tapped Miranda and pointed, and Miranda veered to the base of the cliff and drew rein. Sliding off, they scrambled up an incline and along a narrow lip for forty feet to reach Kaliban, who was on his hands and knees now, peering over the top.

Blue Water Woman set down her rifle and cautiously raised her head above the rim. The Wallanchians had halted less than fifty yards out, and Trent and Culo had dismounted and were scouring the ground for sign, their heads bent low. Shakespeare was on Snowcap, his wrists bound in front of him, at the front of the column next to Duke Viktor Alonzo. She saw him glance toward the canyon's mouth, and it took all her self-control not to try and signal to him.

Miranda was staring at the tall man in blue. Kaliban addressed her in sign, but she was oblivious to all but the handsome royal. Scowling, the hunchback glared at the young man and uttered a low growl which snapped Miranda out of her daze. "I'm sorry," she whispered. "What did you want?"

Kaliban repeated the hand signs.

"He wants to climb higher and hurl boulders down on them if they try to enter the canyon," Miranda translated.

Blue Water Woman envisioned a massive slab of rock smashing onto Shakespeare. "It would endanger my husband. There has to be a better way."

"There is," Miranda said enigmatically.

Just then Kaliban snarled.

Trent and Culo were moving toward the gap, Culo leading their horses by the reins. Every few yards Trent stopped and studied the ground.

Blue Water Woman had met the pair once and was aware of their unsavory reputation. But there was no denying they were skilled trackers, Trent in particular. He was reading sign where there shouldn't be any—on solid rock. The most he had to go by were nicks and scrapes made by the heavy hoofs of Miranda's roan, but it was enough. Soon he was thirty yards out, then twenty. Then fifteen.

"What is taking so long, American?" Duke Viktor Alonzo impatiently demanded. "I thought you claimed we were close?"

Trent didn't bother to glance up. "If you reckon you can do it any faster, your dukeship, be my guest."

"I won't tolerate impudence," Duke Alonzo warned. "Have a care, or you won't receive the money I've promised."

Both Trent and Culo swung around, their fingers on the triggers of their rifles. "We have us a deal, Duke. Me and my friend wouldn't take it kindly were you to try and cheat us out of our due."

The handsome young man in blue intervened. "Both of you will be paid as promised. On that you have my personal guarantee."

"Thanks, Prince," Trent said. "Glad one of you is a man of honor."

Shakespeare burst into laughter while simultaneously kneeing Snowcap past the prince and Duke Alonzo. "Trent, you wouldn't know what honor was if it jumped up and bit you on the ass." He pulled on the reins but didn't bring Snowcap to a complete stop. " 'You are not worth the dust which the rude wind blows in your face,' " he quoted.

"Hold up there!" Duke Alonzo commanded.

Culo had turned and was scanning the rock cliff. Suddenly he tensed and pointed at the entrance to the canyon. "Lookee there, boys! I think that's what we're looking for!"

# Chapter Ten

Shakespeare McNair knew that one of the scouts was bound to spot the opening in the cliff at any moment. So he had contrived to move closer while laughing and taunting Trent. When the duke told him to stop, he acted as if he hadn't heard and kept on going. The next second, when Culo pointed at the gap and yelled, Shakespeare bent low over his saddle and slapped his heels against Snowcap. His intention was to enter the canyon first and race to warn his wife and the Prosperos, but he had only gone a few feet when a remarkable turn of events threw everything into chaos.

Culo had also started toward the opening. He glanced back, grinning merrily, probably thinking of the gold coins that would soon fill his poke. He never saw the huge, dark shape that swept down out of nowhere, smashing him flat and in the process crushing half the bones in his body.

Kaliban flung back his hood, raised his huge arms overhead, and roared in defiance, a nigh-deafening blast of primeval ferocity unmatched by that of any beast alive. A sweep of his steel-

122

sinewed arm sent one of the horses Culo had led toppling.

Snowcap tried to veer aside, but Shakespeare lashed her straight past the hulking hunchback, passing so close he could have reached out and touched the giant's bear-hide robe. Another couple of moments and Shakespeare gained the opening. Slowing, he glanced back and saw the Wallanchians gawking in terror-struck disbelief. Kaliban had placed a massive foot onto Culo's shattered body, pinning the feebly struggling frontiersman facedown. Bending, Kaliban gripped Culo by either side of the head and, with an inhuman surge, ripped Culo's head clean off.

Prince Ferdinand shouted something in Wallanchian.

Kaliban thrust his grisly trophy on high and roared a second time. The headless body was convulsing wildly, a fine red mist spraying from the severed stump.

Shakespeare hurtled into the opening just as the soldiers began to come out of their daze and grabbed for their weapons. "Kaliban, follow me!" he bawled, hoping the hunchback had heard and would heed. Without Kaliban they stood little chance of holding the Wallanchians off for very long.

A shot rang out, then several in succession. Shakespeare feared the worst, but loud, raspy breaths almost on the mare's heels showed that his worry had been premature. The hunchback was right behind him, Culo's head swinging by the hair from his thick fingers.

Again rifles cracked, but ahead of Shakespeare and to the left. As Snowcap brought him into the open, he looked up and saw Blue Water Woman and Miranda Prospero on top of the cliff, reloading their rifles. Hauling on Snowcap's reins, he was off and running before she came to a halt. He almost fell when Kaliban barreled by, nearly knocking him over. As best he could with his wrists tied, he sped up a hand-wide lip of rock to his wife's side.

A soldier lay twenty yards out, motionless. The rest of the troops had dismounted and were hurriedly seeking cover.

"I had to drop one to stop the rest," Blue Water Woman said, tamping a ball and patch down her barrel.

"You're a daisy," Shakespeare said, and wagged his wrists. "Now be a whole bouquet and cut me loose."

Blue Water Woman shifted, showing him her sheath was empty. "I lost it somewhere along the way."

Kaliban had hunkered next to Miranda. Grinning proudly, he cupped Culo's head in both big hands and held it out to her, a gargantuan puppy expecting to be praised for a task well done.

"What made you do that?" Miranda angrily declared while extracting her ramrod from its housing. "I wanted to talk to them! I was going to give myself up and tell them my father died long ago so they would stop looking! But you've ruined everything!"

Kaliban cringed. Whimpering, he raised the head closer to her face, as if he thought she might not have seen it.

"Get that awful thing away from me!" Miranda cried, and slapped the hunchback's hands.

For a few seconds Kaliban was transfixed by shock, his great form stock-still, his good eye betraying hurt beyond measure. Then, venting a tortured howl, he heaved the head out over the cliff, whirled, and bounded down into the canyon with his arms crisscrossed over his face. Culo's head bounced once and rolled to rest near the body it had once been attached to.

Miranda half rose. "Kaliban! Wait! I didn't mean—!"

Out among the boulders beyond the cliff a rifle spanged and a slug whined off the rim inches from her chest. Lunging, Shakespeare yanked her down onto her knees. "Keep low, missy, or Culo won't be the only one losing his head today!" He glanced down into the canyon and saw the hunchback smashing a path through the underbrush on a blind sprint toward the cavern.

Another soldier fired, and a third. The shooting ceased when someone shouted, and for a while deceptive quiet reigned.

Miranda was gazing contritely after the hunchback. "I never

# The Tempest

meant to get him so upset. Damn me for a simpleton! How could I forget how sensitive he is?"

"You can talk to him later and smooth things over," Shakespeare said, sitting up. For now, they had a much more important matter to attend to. "I suggest the two of you hightail it back. I'll stay here and hold the duke's men off as long as I can."

"A gallant gesture, Mr. McNair," Miranda said, "but retreat is a last resort. We must exploit our advantage. From up here we can pick off Alonzo's men if they rush the opening, but they will have a hard time hitting us."

Shakespeare was willing to concede that Miranda had a point, but only if the soldiers tried to reach the canyon in twos and threes. A concerted charge by all the troops at once would be unstoppable. Wriggling his bound wrists at her, he said, "How about you? You wouldn't happen to have a knife handy, would you?"

Miranda absently drew an ivory-handled dirk and sliced the hemp. "Here, take this." She shoved a pistol into his grasp.

"I wish I had my own guns," Shakespeare groused. With his Hawken he could shoot the whiskers off a bobcat at a hundred yards. Well, an ear, anyway.

"Did you take a good look at the soldiers I shot?" Blue Water Woman said.

"What's that got to do with the price of tea in China?" Shakespeare said, and inched an eyeball to the rim. The man lay in a disjointed heap forty feet from the cliff, a red pool spreading outward from his red uniform. "He's dead? So what?"

"Perhaps you should send to St. Louis for spectacles," Blue Water Woman said. "Look closer. Open your eyes this time."

Shakespeare studied the body and chuckled. Lying beside the trooper were two rifles, one a European model, the other his prized Hawken. "You shot the man who was carrying my guns?" Now all they had to do was wait until nightfall and he could sneak out there and get them.

Blue Water Woman smiled coyly. "It seemed like the wise thing to do."

"I knew there was a reason I married you," Shakespeare quipped.

"Quiet!" Miranda urged, and pointed. "Look there! What do you make of that? It's the tall one in blue."

"Prince Ariel Ferdinand," Shakespeare said. The king's son had risen and boldly stepped into the open, his hands out from his sides to show he was not holding a firearm. His hat was missing, and the breeze ruffled his hair as he slowly advanced.

"Ariel?" Miranda repeated as if the name struck a chord.

"He told me the two of you played together when you were knee-high to grasshoppers," Shakespeare related.

"I remember now!" Miranda cried. "Dimly, in bits and fragments, but I definitely remember. My father spent months at the capital at one point as a guest of the king, and the prince and I were together every waking hour." Impulsively, she leaped to her feet and extended her arms to show that she, too, wasn't holding a gun.

"Damn," Shakespeare muttered. Grabbing her rifle, he slid past her for a clearer view of the boulders and tucked the stock to his shoulder to cover her. "Are you trying to get yourself killed, girl?"

Miranda either didn't hear or didn't care. Her face had lit up like a lantern and she was smiling warmly. Out of habit, in English she asked, "Have you led any girls around by the hand lately, Ariel?"

The prince was feasting his eyes on her, his smile every bit as radiant. "Miranda Prospero. After all these years. And lovelier by far than when you toddled around in diapers."

Miranda blushed beautifully. "You have grown some, yourself, Ariel. The crown will rest nobly on so handsome a brow."

Shakespeare almost snickered out loud. He had to remind himself that young love was a glorious love, prone to intoxicating extremes.

Prince Ferdinand halted ten yards out and glanced at the scarlet trickling from the stump of Culo's bull neck. "Would that we had met under different circumstances. What *was* the thing that slew this poor fellow?"

"My brother," Miranda said, her smile fading by degrees as reality reasserted itself. "Or as close to a brother as I have in this world."

Confusion etched the prince. "As I recall, you were an only child. I would like to hear more of this. That is, if we can sit down and discuss the situation in a mature, civilized manner?"

"I would like nothing better," Miranda said. "But I tell you now, I will not surrender myself or my father to that murderer you ride with. I would rather die first."

"Let's have no talk of death, particularly yours," Prince Ferdinand said. "As for Duke Alonzo, I ask only that you hear me out. There is much you do not know, and which, when conveyed, will set your heart at ease and prove my presence here is not as your enemy but as an arbiter of justice."

Miranda glanced at Blue Water Woman. "Do I trust him? Do we let him into the canyon or spurn his offer?"

"What does your heart say?"

With no hesitation whatsoever, Miranda called down, "You, and you alone, may enter. You must do so unarmed. But you have my personal assurance no harm will befall you."

Shakespeare nudged the countess's leg and whispered, "Whoa there! Tell him to bring my rifle and pistols. My knife, too, while he's at it."

His request was relayed. The prince reflected a few moments, then turned to the boulders. "Duke Alonzo, you heard?"

"Every word, my prince! But I urge you not to trust her. She is the devious offspring of a notorious thief. They only want to get you in their power so they can hold you hostage and bend us to their will!"

Shakespeare thought it interesting that while the prince had bravely shown himself, the duke remained concealed.

"I remind you, Duke Alonzo, that I am in command," Prince Ferdinand said. "My father has given me a commission, and I will faithfully execute it to the best of my ability." Sliding his pistol from its holster, he dropped it at his feet. The same with his saber.

"I beg you to reconsider! I cannot protect you once you are out of my sight."

"I have Miranda's pledge, and that is sufficient for me." Prince Ferdinand strode to the dead soldier. "Two men have already perished. If I can avert further loss of life, I have an obligation to do so."

Alonzo's bearded visage rose into sight, partially screened by a jutting spur of rock. Shakespeare fixed a bead on it but couldn't get a clear shot. "Please, my prince! You know not what manner of lies and treachery they will spout! Let me give the order and my men will rush them and end this farce once and for all."

"No!" Ferdinand barked, and resorted to the Wallanchian language.

Miranda translated. "He is ordering them to stay where they are until he returns. No one is to fire, no one is to come after him. Anyone who fails to obey will be severely punished." Her eyes had never once left the prince. "He has a marvelous commanding presence about him, doesn't he?" she remarked.

"I suppose," Shakespeare said, "but his nose is a mite too big for my tastes."

Prince Ferdinand gathered up the Hawken, both flintlock pistols, and the Green River knife. His arms full, he turned his back on the boulders.

Shakespeare stiffened. A rifle barrel had poked from the shadows, pointed at the young prince. He was going to yell a warning, but someone—the duke, possibly—said something and the barrel was withdrawn.

Miranda crouched and turned. "If the two of you are willing to stand guard, I will escort Ariel to the cavern."

"Fine by me," Shakespeare said, shoving her rifle at her. "Just so I get my guns back before the two of you waltz off to make cow eyes at each other."

"Cow eyes?"

"Pay no attention to him, Miranda," Blue Water Woman said. "He lost his sense of humor many winters ago, about the time his hair turned white."

"But my hair has always been white." Shakespeare stepped into her snare, and his wife's tinkly mirth followed him down the cliff.

The prince took his time winding through the gap, and Miranda availed herself of the opportunity to smooth her clothes, brush dust and lint from her skirt, wipe a scuff mark from the tip of a shoe, and run her hands through her hair.

"Would you like a twig to pick your teeth clean?" Shakespeare asked.

Miranda was about to make a tart retort when Prince Ariel Ferdinand came around the last bend. Visibly softening, Miranda said softly, "Thank you, Ariel, for trusting me. I, too, wish we had met again other different circumstances. It pains me to think how poorly you must regard me."

The prince reacted as if he had been smacked. "Nothing could be further from the truth. To be honest, I have thought of little else except those happy days we shared ever since my father charged me with the chore of finding you and settling a mystery that has gnawed at him for two decades."

Shakespeare skipped over to reclaim his hardware. "If you don't mind," he said. He might as well have said it to the cliff. Ferdinand had eyes only for Miranda, which was just as well, since she had eyes only for him.

"What mystery would that be?" the young woman inquired.

"The enigma of what really happened in Prospero Province. My father always thought highly of your grandfather and was saddened greatly at his death. Then came Duke Alonzo's charge of embezzlement and high treason against Stephen."

"Vicious slanders!" Miranda declared.

"My father had his doubts," Prince Ferdinand said. "But when the two of you fled, it appeared to confirm the duke's accusations. The evidence was clear-cut, yet my father had been troubled by grave doubts. He's always harbored a suspicion that there was more to the affair than the circumstances bore out."

Shakespeare backed off, his pistols under his belt, his Green River knife snug in its sheath where it belonged, the Hawken once again his.

Miranda came forward until she was a finger's width from the prince, her lovely upturned face the essence of innocence and sincerity. "As God is my witness, the only reason my father fled was to save us from the duke's paid assassins. Alonzo had already had my grandfather slain, and my father didn't want us sharing his fate."

"Viktor had your grandfather killed? In the name of heaven, why?"

"Greed. Vile, wicked greed. When a count is disgraced, the duke he serves under always absorbs the count's holdings into his own. Isn't that the tradition?"

Prince Ferdinand stroked his square jaw. "Surely there is deviltry afoot. I must talk to your father and hear his account of those long-ago events."

Miranda gave a little bow and motioned to the south. "After you. Our less-than-humble home is at the other end of this canyon, in a cavern."

"You have been living in a hole in the ground?" Prince Ferdinand said, appalled. He started off, then glanced at Shakespeare. "Pardon my manners. Have you any words to impart about this situation?"

Shakespeare couldn't resist. " 'The son of Priam, a true knight, not yet mature, yet matchless, firm of word, speaking in deeds and deedless in his tongue, not soon provoked nor being provoked soon calmed. His heart and hand open and both free.' "

Confusion beset the prince again. "By my word, wasn't that Shakespeare?"

"Of a sort," Shakespeare said.

"But what does that have to do with my question?" Ferdinand said. "I was asking for your thoughts on all this."

"Oh," Shakespeare said. "In that case . . ." He paused. " 'All the world's a stage, and all the men and women merely players. They have their exits and their entrances, and one man in his time plays many parts.' "

The prince looked at Miranda. "Is this fellow touched in the head? Why does he answer me with quotes and more quotes?"

"He thinks he is a book." Miranda clasped Ferdinand's hand. "Come. We'll take my horse. I don't trust the duke to hold off forever."

Shakespeare grinned and waved as they galloped away, but neither returned the favor. Pivoting, he climbed to the cliff's crest and hunkered beside his wife. "The lovebirds have gone to talk to her pa. What has the blackguard been up to?"

"Duke Alonzo?" Blue Water Woman's chin rested on a forearm and her rifle lay crosswise below the rim. "I haven't seen or heard him, but one of the soldiers has been running from boulder to boulder."

"Passing on orders, I'll bet." Shakespeare dared a peek and glimpsed the soldier she referred to darting from one spot to another.

"What were Miranda and Prince Ferdinand talking about?"

"He's fixing to propose before the day is done," Shakespeare said. "They'll go off to Wallanchia after this is over and have a royal wedding. Ten years from now, he'll be king and she'll be queen and they'll have a passel of sprouts scampering underfoot, and they'll go on to live happily ever after."

"They said all that?"

"Not exactly, no, but that was the general drift."

Blue Water Woman impishly tweaked his cheek. "Has anyone ever mentioned you are incurably romantic?"

"As afflictions go, it beats jaundice and the measles all hollow." Shakespeare leaned back and admired her. "When this is over, you and I should go up to that high-country lake we like and spend a week or two relaxing."

"At this time of year? The nights are cold at that altitude."

"Nitpick, nitpick, nitpick," Shakespeare said, and leered lecherously. "I'll keep you plenty warm, don't you worry."

Blue Water Woman grew serious. "How is it a man with as many wrinkles as you have still has an interest in cuddling? Most men your age have given up on it."

"Dunderheads and dunces. The day I give up on one of the prime joys of life is the day they plant me six feet under." Shakespeare pushed his beaver hat back on his head. "When a person stops enjoying life, they might as well find a shovel and dig their own grave. Their juices wither and they turn into grumpy old prunes, and before you know it, they're sitting in a rocking chair all day waiting for the Lord to claim them."

"You sit in your rocking chair a lot," Blue Water Woman baited him.

"But I always make time for cuddling." Shakespeare would have expanded on the topic if not for a hail from below.

"Can you hear me up there? This is Duke Viktor Alonzo!"

Blue Water woman gripped her rifle. "What does he want?"

"Probably an invite to the wedding." Shakespeare cupped his hands to his mouth and hollered, "We hear you, sidewinder."

"Sidewinder?" Alonzo responded. "I do not know that term."

"I can give you some idea," Shakespeare shouted. "Have you ever walked across a cow pasture?"

"On occasion, yes."

"Ever step in those round piles the cows leave?"

"You are a humorous man, American," the duke said, but he didn't sound amused. "Now humor me and ask the prince to show himself so I might know he is all right."

"He's just fine," Shakespeare said, "but he's not here at the moment. Miranda and him rode off to see her father."

"Rode off?" Duke Alonzo sounded alarmed. "No one said anything about him leaving. How do I know you haven't slain him and are lying to me?"

"You'll have to take my word for it."

"Your word?" Duke Alonzo's brittle laugh was contemptuous. "I would sooner trust a—what did you just call it? Ah, yes. I would sooner trust a sidewinder."

The duke fell quiet and Shakespeare figured that was the end of it, but two minutes later Alonzo shouted again.

"I would like to send two of my men in to verify the prince is safe. They will come unarmed with their hands in the air."

"No," Shakespeare answered. The only way to verify it was to take them to the cavern, and he wasn't leaving his wife to guard the canyon entrance alone.

"Only one man, then," the duke insisted. "What can it hurt for one solitary man?"

Blue Water Woman had not been Shakespeare's wife for so long for nothing. "I do not mind staying by myself, husband. Leave Snowcap here. If they rush the opening, I will ride back to warn all of you."

Shakespeare shook his head. "What if they attack on horseback? You'd never reach the cavern. No, we're staying put."

Duke Alonzo wouldn't let it drop. "What do you say, American? On my word as a gentleman, the soldier will behave and do whatever you request of him. What can be fairer?" He stopped, but only for ten seconds or so. "Try to understand my position. King Ferdinand entrusted me with the safekeeping of his son, and it is not a responsibility I take lightly."

"The prince will be back soon!" Or so Shakespeare hoped.

"That is not good enough. I was instructed to never let him out of my sight. I gave in this once, but only because I thought he would not go far. Now you inform me he is gone. Can you blame me for being disturbed?"

"He is most persistent, this duke," Blue Water Woman said.

133

A little *too* persistent, Shakespeare thought. Prince Ferdinand had commanded Alonzo to stay put and not do a thing. Obviously, the king's orders took precedence, but the prince's should count for something.

"How about if *I* come instead?" the duke yelled. "Me, and me alone. Merely to satisfy myself the prince is not in jeopardy."

Annoyance filled Shakespeare. The man didn't know when to leave well enough be, prattling on and on like he was. Shakespeare would never have taken the duke for the gabby type. Alonzo was more a man of action; to him, talking was a means to an end, not an end in itself. *A means to an end.* The phrase resounded in Shakespeare's head, along with a sudden suspicion. With all the jabbering the duke was doing, it was almost as if Alonzo *wanted* to keep them talking to distract them from something else. But what? The soldiers were still behind the boulders. No one could reach the canyon without being seen. Not from the front, anyhow. Shakespeare hadn't even considered the possibility that there might be another way in. Perhaps by working around to either side *and scaling the cliff!*

Whirling, Shakespeare scanned the crest—and there was Trent, fifty feet to the east on bended knee, his rifle pressed to a shoulder, taking deliberate aim.

# Chapter Eleven

"Get down!" Shakespeare McNair bawled, and flung himself at his wife. He couldn't tell which of them Trent was aiming at, but he would rather take a bullet than have Blue Water Woman take one. His left arm looped around her waist as he covered her body with his own and threw her down much harder than he intended, so hard she cried out. Trent's rifle cracked, and the slug whined off rock near where her head had been.

If Shakespeare hadn't acted, Trent would have splattered her brains all over the cliff. Enraged, he heaved onto his knees and swiveled at the hips. Trent was drawing a long-barreled pistol. Both of them snapped their weapons up, both took rapid aim, but it was the Hawken that boomed first, and it was Trent whose skull exploded in a shower of gore. Trent tried to rise, but his limbs erupted in spasms and he toppled onto his face, his body flopping and thrashing and leaving a wide red smear.

Trent's initial shot had been the signal Duke Viktor Alonzo and the Wallanchian soldiers were waiting for. At a roar from Alonzo the twenty-two remaining soldiers simultaneously rose up from hiding and charged toward the mouth of the canyon. They voiced a collective cry as they charged, yelling in Wallanchian. Fully half unleashed a volley at the top of the cliff.

Shakespeare's head was above the rim, and he threw himself flat as a swarm of leaden bees buzzed through the air and pinged off stone. Grabbing Blue Water Woman by the wrist, he shouted, "We have to light a shuck!" and rolled toward the lip that would take them to the bottom. They descended recklessly, aware that if they didn't reach the mare before the soldiers reached them, they were as good as dead. All went well until they were near the bottom. Then Shakespeare's left moccasin slipped out from under him on the smooth surface and he crashed onto his backside. Excruciating pain lanced up his spine, and for a few seconds he couldn't move. Blue Water Woman had to hook her arm under his and forcefully haul him to his feet to get him moving again.

Snowcap was waiting, head high, ears pricked toward the opening. Suddenly she whinnied and stomped the ground.

The fleetest of the soldiers was already through the gap, a young trooper with peach fuzz on his chin. He was fast but he was green as grass, for when he saw Snowcap he made right for her and reached out to snag her reins instead of looking to his left as he should have done. Only after Snowcap shied and he missed his hold did he think to turn toward the cliff and bring his rifle into play.

By then Blue Water Woman had her own rifle leveled. She stroked the trigger, and the young soldier was kicked backward as if by an invisible sledgehammer. Mouth gaping, he tottered a dozen feet and sprawled to the dust, a new hole between his eyes.

"More will come," Blue Water Woman said, lending Shakespeare another hand. "Hurry, husband."

Shakespeare was trying, but his legs weren't working as they should. Through sheer force of will he smothered the pain and ran the last eight or nine yards. His wife reached Snowcap first and lithely swung up. Normally when they rode double he was in front, but under the circumstances he wasn't about to quibble. Accepting the hand she lowered, he jumped and straddled the mare's back.

More soldiers streamed into the open as Blue Water Woman reined Snowcap around and launched into a gallop. Rifles cracked in uneven cadence, four, five, six of them, and Shakespeare heard a ball whizz past his ear.

Blue Water Woman bent low over Snowcap's neck to make herself harder to hit. Following suit, Shakespeare pressed against his wife. Snowcap flew flat out, her mane and tail streaming, her hoofs churning clods of dirt and grass. He was concerned about her leg, but the mare never broke stride. Within seconds they were in heavy brush, and although more shots pealed off the canyon walls none came anywhere near them.

"We are safe now," Blue Water Woman said, uncurling.

"For the moment," Shakespeare responded. It wouldn't take Duke Alonzo's bunch long to gather up their mounts and give chase.

"We will inform Prince Ferdinand," Blue Water Woman said over a shoulder. "He will put a stop to this."

Maybe, Shakespeare thought. And maybe not. Duke Alonzo had just disobeyed a direct order. What was to stop him from doing so again? And, too, Shakespeare didn't like how the duke kept referring to the soldiers as "his." There could be more to the duke's actions than concern for the prince.

Shakespeare repeatedly glanced back but saw no sign of pursuit. Soon they came to the tree where the roan was tethered. They climbed down, and Blue Water Woman went to tie the mare's reins to a low limb.

"Don't bother. We're taking the horses with us." Shakespeare undid the roan's reins.

"Into the cavern?" Blue Water Woman said doubtfully.

"We don't want the duke to get his hands on them, do we?"

Shakespeare took the lead, hustling rapidly along the path, half expecting at any moment to be challenged by Kaliban. But the hunchback didn't appear, and as they entered the tunnel voices reached him, the prince and the Prosperos speaking in Wallanchian. To go by the low laughter that punctuated their conversation, they were on very friendly terms.

The cavern's roof arched over Shakespeare's head. He guided the roan to the pool, wrapped the reins around a rock outcropping, and hurried on, his wife only a few steps behind. A lantern had been lit and placed on the long table. Count Prospero was in his usual chair, Miranda and Prince Ferdinand in others near him.

"Shakespeare? Blue Water Woman?" Miranda said in surprise, rising. "I thought you were keeping watch."

"We were," Shakespeare said, and briefly recounted the clash, ending with "The duke will be here any minute. If there's another way out of this canyon, now's the time to share the secret."

"There isn't," Count Prospero said anxiously. "Alonzo has us right where he wants us, trapped like wild animals."

Prince Ferdinand was a study in indignation. "How dare Viktor disobey me! I will assume direct command and end these hostilities before they go any further." He started toward the tunnel.

"Hold up a second, hos," Shakespeare said, gripping the heir apparent's arm. "Tell me something before you march off in a huff to get yourself killed."

"Killed? By Wallanchian soldiers?" Prince Ferdinand snorted. "My father is their sovereign liege. To a man they are loyal to the crown. They would no more harm me than they would harm the king."

"Just answer me one thing," Shakespeare persisted. "*Whose* soldiers are they, exactly?"

"I'm not sure I understand," the prince said. "All Wallanchian soldiers are enlisted in the service of the king, no matter which dukedom or province they hail from."

The prince tried to walk on, but again Shakespeare restrained him. "Bear with me a second, junior. Something the duke said has been gnawing at me. If all those soldiers are in service to your pa, why does the duke keep calling those men 'his'?"

"I suppose because they are from his dukedom. Members of his personal guard. He handpicked them to accompany us to America." Prince Ferdinand shrugged loose. "I fail to see where that has any significance. They still took an oath of loyalty to the crown and would never lift a finger against a member of the royal household. Now, if you will excuse me, I must set matters aright."

"I'll tag along," Shakespeare volunteered. Someone had to protect the prince from his own stupidity. To the women he said, "Gather up all the guns and ammo we have. Bring them over to the tunnel. Oath or no oath, we just might have a fight on our hands."

Shakespeare hastened to catch up to the prince. "When the duke and his boys get here, it might be best not to show yourself."

Prince Ferdinand seemed amused. "What do you expect me to do? Call out to them from hiding?"

"That would be nice, yes."

"I am a prince of the realm," Ferdinand declared. "I do not cower before my own troops. It is beneath my dignity to contemplate so craven an act."

"Is it beneath your dignity to die?"

Prince Ferdinand dismissed the notion with a gesture and tramped on out the tunnel, his head high, his arms swinging military-fashion, the living embodiment of royal demeanor.

Sighing, Shakespeare tagged along. Almost too late he remembered he needed to reload the Hawken and proceeded to do so while walking. He had to slow a bit to pour the powder down the muzzle, which allowed the prince to pull ahead. By the time he finished and doubled his speed, the monarch-to-be was past the boulders and nearing the tree where the horses were usually tied.

Huffing from the exertion, Shakespeare said, "Slow up there, youngster. Don't be in such an all-fired rush to be made a jack-ass of."

"I beg your pardon?" Prince Ferdinand halted and smoothed a sleeve. "While I find myself liking you, McNair, you have a penchant for taking liberties."

"How so?"

"Familiarity, sir. It is rude to be so familiar with someone you hardly know. In my country you would be considered a vulgar misfit and be shunned by cultured citizens everywhere."

"You keep forgetting you're in my country now," Shakespeare said. "And in America we've refined being vulgar to a fine art. We wallow in being crude, like hogs in a feed trough, and make no apologies to anyone."

"Rather boorish, don't you think?"

Shakespeare heard the distant drum of hoofs; the soldiers were on their way.

"Only to stuffed shirts who can't see the world past the ends of their noses. Americans don't kowtow to high-and-mighty types who think they're better than the rest of humanity. We take life as it comes and live it to the fullest."

A cloud of dust billowed skyward, heralding the thunderous arrival of Duke Viktor Alonzo at the head of the twenty-one surviving troopers. When the duke spied the prince, he raised a gloved hand and slowed the column from a trot to a walk.

Prince Ferdinand clasped his hands behind his back, awaiting them. "I would like to discuss this further with you later. To be frank, your people and your culture fascinate me no end."

"If we live, I'll be happy to oblige." Shakespeare stepped a few feet to the left so if he had to shoot the prince wouldn't be in the way.

"Of course we'll live," Prince Ferdinand scoffed. "I keep telling you these men are loyal to the crown."

"And I keep telling *you* that only a dunderhead puts a fox in charge of the henhouse."

"How is that again?" the prince asked, but any answer was forestalled by the clattering arrival of the column. In a swirl of dust they reined to a stop mere yards away. Without preliminaries the young prince took a step and sternly demanded in English, for Shakespeare's benefit, "Viktor, what is the meaning of this? I gave you specific orders not to leave your positions."

Duke Viktor Alonzo pursed his lips and casually flicked dust from his red jacket.

"Didn't you hear me?" Prince Ferdinand prompted. "I asked you a question."

"I heard, you popinjay," Duke Alonzo quietly responded.

The prince started. "What did you call me?"

Smirking, Duke Alonzo glanced at Shakespeare. "The truth still eludes him, doesn't it? It would be hilarious were it not so pathetic. To think, this man might one day have been the ruler of Wallanchia. We might as well install a block of wood."

A crack appeared in Prince Ferdinand's confident bearing. "Do you realize you could be tried for treason for talking to me like that? When my father is informed—"

"Your father won't *be* informed, you pathetic cretin," Duke Alonzo stated. "When I return, I will tell him you were slain by Count Prospero. A royal funeral will be held, and the country will be in official mourning for a week with all the flags at half-mast."

"But that would be a lie!" Prince Ferdinand declared. Glancing at the soldiers, his confidence flowered anew and he addressed them in Wallanchian—a string of commands, judging by his tone.

No one moved. The soldiers sat their mounts like statues. A few snickered. A few grinned.

Prince Ferdinand took another stride and addressed them again in his native language, longer this time, accenting his speech with hard gestures.

141

Shakespeare glued his gaze to the duke; Alonzo was the one who would initiate the fireworks when Alonzo deemed the time ripe.

The young prince was crimson with anger. His hand lowered to the flap covering his holster.

"I wouldn't, were I you," Duke Alonzo said in English. "If I so much as snap my fingers, you will be riddled where you stand." He bent forward and grinned wickedly. "Have you forgotten? These men are from *my* dukedom. I chose each one, not on the basis of how loyal they are to you, but on how loyal they are to *me*. They will do whatever I ask of them."

"You planned this all along?" Prince Ferdinand said in dawning dismay.

"At last. A glimmer of intelligence." Alonzo loosened his left boot from its stirrup and shifted in the saddle, sliding his left knee up onto the pommel. "Clearly, I need to spell it out for you. You see, Ariel, Count Prospero never diverted a single cent from the royal coffers. He would never betray the king's trust. But it was ridiculously simple to concoct evidence he had." Alonzo grinned. "Prospero helped out immensely by fleeing the country after I made certain he received word the king had sent a magistrate to take him into custody. Your father naturally assumed an innocent man wouldn't run. It never occurred to him the count might have another reason."

"What would that have been?" Prince Ferdinand asked coldly.

Alonzo chortled, savoring his triumph. "Poor Prospero fled because he was afraid I might do to him as I did to his father."

"So what the count just told me is true," Prince Ferdinand said. "You had his father murdered by base assassins."

"Prospero is nearby? Where?" Duke Alonzo sat up and scoured the vegetation, but from where he sat the cavern wasn't visible. "I can't wait to greet him in person."

Prince Ferdinand turned slightly, his fingers slowly easing under his holster's flap. "There are a few things I don't yet comprehend," he remarked.

"Only a few?" Alonzo said sarcastically.

"Yes. For instance, why didn't you object when my father insisted I come to America with you?"

The duke's countenance twisted in contempt. "How big an idiot do you take me for? I knew your father had doubts about Prospero. His chambermaid is secretly in my employ, and she reported a conversation between the two of you in which your father praised the Prosperos for their faithfulness and speculated there might be more to their case." Alonzo scowled. "The king always suspected me of complicity, but he had no proof. So he sent you along to uncover the truth. Little did he realize I would use this occasion, as the Americans like to say, to slay two birds with one stone."

The young prince froze. "You truly intend to murder me, Viktor?"

Alonzo straightened. "You, the Prosperos, the McNairs, and the creature that slew our scout if it interferes. In one fell swoop I will wipe the slate clean. The cloud of suspicion that has been hanging over me for decades will be gone."

"You won't deceive the king," Prince Ferdinand declared. "He will know you were to blame."

"Oh, he might harbor a few suspicions, but he won't lift a finger against the most powerful duke in his kingdom, not when I have all these witnesses." Duke Alonzo motioned at the soldiers. "Each of whom, by the way, has been promised a stipend of a thousand a year for the rest of their lives for keeping their mouths shut."

"A bribe, you mean," the prince angrily rasped. "These men are a disgrace to their uniforms."

"Silence is golden, however ensured," Duke Alonzo said. "And you shouldn't be so quick to criticize. You have brought this on yourself."

"Now I'm to blame for my own murder," the prince said resentfully. "Is there no end to your delusions?"

"Listen to the kettle call the pot black." Duke Alonzo lowered his leg. "Killing you was always a last resort, a contingency if you learned the truth. I tried my best to spare you, to keep you from talking to the girl or the count. I *begged* you, if you'll recall, not to go meet with her. But you refused to listen. You had to do it your way, and thereby set the wheels of your own death in motion."

"Justify it all you want. You are a callous killer, and if there is any justice in the cosmos, one day you will reap the results of the evil you have sown." Prince Ferdinand's fingertips brushed his flintlock.

"Perhaps," the duke retorted, "but you won't be around to see it."

"Maybe I will!" Ferdinand cried, and clawed at his pistol. He drew quickly, smoothly, cocking the hammer as his hand swept up and out, but at the same instant half a dozen soldiers did likewise.

Shakespeare had anticipated the prince's rash act, and sprang, slamming into Ferdinand and propelling him toward the tree at the very moment the prince fired. The shot intended for the duke went wild, and the six shots intended for the prince cleaved the space he had occupied.

Shakespeare and the prince fell to their knees behind the wide trunk, momentarily shielded. He heard the bole thud to multiple rounds as Duke Alonzo bellowed in Wallanchian. Hoofs clattered, and Shakespeare peered out to see the duke and the majority of soldiers seeking cover. One man, however, braver or less intelligent than the rest, let out with a whoop and spurred his mount forward. He had a pistol in one hand, his reins in the other.

Shakespeare drew one of his own flintlocks. He centered the front sight on the soldier's chest and fired a heartbeat sooner than the soldier did. Catapulted backward, the Wallanchian tumbled head over heels off the rump of his animal and thumped to earth like a flung sack of potatoes.

Prince Ferdinand had risen. His outrage at being thwarted

eclipsed his reason, and he railed, "What on earth got into you, McNair? I had him, had him dead to rights, and you spoiled my shot!"

"Gripe about it later," Shakespeare said. Seizing the younger man by the arm, he shoved him toward the trail to the tunnel. "After you run like hell!"

For a moment the prince was riveted by indecision, but only for a moment. Pistols and rifles blasted in unison, chewing the trunk to bits and missing him by a cat's whisker. For all his courage and air of superiority, the young prince was no fool. Pivoting on a boot heel, he sprinted into the boulders.

Shakespeare shoved the spent pistol under his belt. Backpedaling, he palmed the other one, thumbed back the hammer, and sighted on a soldier who presented the greatest threat—a stocky trooper fixing a bead on the prince's back. Shakespeare's flintlock spewed lead and smoke, and at the retort, the soldier screamed, pressed both hands to his ravaged right eye, and keeled over.

Duke Viktor Alonzo was bellowing orders in Wallanchian, his yells drowned out by the shouts of his soldiers, the squealing of their horses, and the sustained smattering of gunfire.

Suddenly seven or eight soldiers fired all at once, and how it was Shakespeare wasn't hit, he would never know. Slugs whined and ricocheted on all sides as he flew up the path. Several clipped whangs off his buckskins. One nicked his left arm. Not deep, not enough to draw blood, but sufficient to send pain coursing through him.

Some of the soldiers started in pursuit, while others reloaded.

Up ahead, Prince Ferdinand was almost to the tunnel. Waiting in the opening were Blue Water Woman and Miranda Prospero, who had an extra rifle she tossed to the prince.

Shakespeare reached them, whirled, and sank onto his right knee. "Get down! Fire when I say to!" he hollered. None too soon, the three of them imitated his example. Hardly had they done so than the foremost soldiers charged out from among the boulders.

"Fire!" Shakespeare shouted, suiting action to words. Their four rifles discharged almost in the faces of their foes. Four soldiers dropped in their tracks, a fifth was wounded by a ball that passed through the man in front of him, and the rest spun and retreated, unwilling to share the fate of their comrades.

"Into the tunnel!" Shakespeare urged. He let them precede him, his whole body prickling as if from a rash for the few moments he was exposed and vulnerable. Hugging the left-hand wall, he backed into the cavern and commenced to reload.

The others were already doing so.

"How many do you think are left?" Prince Ferdinand wondered.

"More than enough to turn us into sieves," Shakespeare acknowledged. His best guess was fifteen, maybe sixteen, counting the duke.

The women had piled spare ammo pouches and powder horns just inside the cavern, enough to hold off a sizable force. But Shakespeare couldn't see Alonzo trying a frontal assault. Too many soldiers would die. No, he figured Alonzo would wait them out. *Starve* them out, to be more accurate. They had plenty of water but not much food. In four or five days, a week at the most, they would be too weak to offer much resistance.

"If only Kaliban were here," Miranda said as she opened her ammo pouch and fished out a ball and patch. "I shouldn't have slapped him like I did. He's like a child when his feelings are hurt. He runs off and sulks."

"Where does he go?" Shakespeare asked, his attention on a commotion at the far end of the tunnel.

"I've never been able to find out."

A shadow materialized on the right-hand wall and rapidly swelled in size, assuming gigantic proportions. "It's him!" Miranda cried, but Shakespeare knew better. The shadow was a trick of the light, the result of sunlight silhouetting someone just outside the entrance. He could guess who it was.

"Can you hear me in there?" Duke Viktor Alonzo shouted.

"We hear you!" Prince Ferdinand responded, and stepped into the opening.

"Are you trying to get yourself rubbed out?" Shakespeare yanked on the prince's blue coat, hauling him back. "Haven't you learned your lesson yet?"

Duke Alonzo's icy laughter rippled off the walls. "So what have we here? A cave? I imagine this is the only exit, or we wouldn't be having this little talk." His laughter acquired a vicious note. "How brilliant. You've boxed yourselves in and are completely at my mercy. If only all my enemies were so accommodating!"

"We will resist with our dying breaths!" Prince Ferdinand countered. "And we have more than enough guns and ammunition to hold you off a good long while!"

Alonzo's chuckle was a masterpiece of scorn. "My dear boy, have you so soon forgotten? Do you honestly expect me to waste more of my men or my time when I can end this farce once and for all with one of the casks?"

"Casks?" Shakespeare said.

"My word!" Prince Ferdinand blurted. "I forgot! We brought along two casks of black powder rigged with fuses in case we ran into large bands of hostiles."

*A cask of powder!* Shakespeare's breath caught in his throat. All Alonzo had to do was have one of the casks tossed far enough into the tunnel and the resultant explosion would bring tons of rock and earth crashing down around their heads.

# *Chapter Twelve*

Shakespeare McNair crouched low and darted from the right side of the tunnel to the left, hoping for a glimpse of the sadistic killer who cruelly intended to snuff out the lives of five human beings as cavalierly as if they were candle wicks. It occurred to him that while Kaliban was considered a hideous monster by those who didn't know him, the true monster was Duke Viktor Alonzo. The man reeked of depraved evil. Where Kaliban was deformed outwardly, Alonzo was deformed deep in his soul. The duke was a twisted, calculating brute who took perverse delight in the pain and suffering of others. Try as Shakespeare might, however, he couldn't spot their tormentor, and after a moment Alonzo called out to them again.

"This works out even better than I planned! Once I've buried you under this mountain, no one will ever find your bodies. I needn't worry that years from now your skeletons will be discovered and possibly identified by the royal crest on the ring the prince wears."

Prince Ferdinand looked down at his hand and frowned.

"And now that I think about it," Alonzo gloated on, "a whole new opportunity has opened up for me. With Ariel gone, his younger brother, Uriel, is next in line to the throne. Were something to happen to him the king would have no direct heirs. An enterprising duke—myself, say—might be able to arrange events so that one day the Wallanchian crown adorns my forehead."

"Never!" Prince Ferdinand responded. Quivering with fury, he made as if to rush out. This time it was Miranda who stopped him.

"Never say never, Ariel," Alonzo mocked him. "Life is full of limitless possibilities to those who know how to seize them."

"I would rather die than see you usurp the crown!"

Duke Alonzo thought the comment worthy of gruff mirth. "My dear boy, you are going to die anyway. And there is absolutely nothing you can do to prevent it."

"That's where he's wrong," Shakespeare said so only his wife, the prince, and Miranda heard. "He doesn't know we have the horses. We'll mount up, two to an animal. When I say so, we'll ride hell-bent for leather. With a little luck we can break through the soldiers and make our getaway."

"What about my father?" Miranda whispered. "I'm not leaving him behind."

"We'll hide him and come back later," Shakespeare proposed.

"You call that a plan?" Miranda said. "What if the duke finds him? Or blows up the cavern anyway to spite us? No, you'll have to come up with something else."

There *was* nothing else, Shakespeare reflected, other than a suicidal charge that would get them all killed. He looked to his wife for support, but she was deep in thought. About what, he couldn't guess.

"Viktor!" the prince called out. "I would like to make you an offer."

"You have nothing I could possibly want," Alonzo said flatly. Movement at the far end hinted to Shakespeare that the soldiers were readying a cask. Something had to be done, and done quickly.

"I have myself!" Prince Ferdinand said. "I will walk out and let you do to me as you will if you agree to let these people live."

"No!" Miranda declared.

She need not have worried. Duke Alonzo seethed with disdain. "How disgustingly noble of you! But why should I bargain for lives already mine to do with as I please? I made the mistake of leaving a witness alive once. I will not make the same mistake twice."

Shakespeare dropped onto his belly. "Stay here!" he whispered, and snaked outward, the Hawken in front of him. Shadow shrouded the tunnel, so he deemed it likely he would spot the soldiers before they spotted him. Crawling swiftly, he soon beheld four men at the tunnel's end, just to the right of the opening.

Duke Alonzo, hands on his hips, was overseeing the work of two soldiers preparing to light a cask. Both had squatted, and one was unfastening a saddlebag. From the pouch he took a container of matches and opened it.

Shakespeare wasn't sure if they were lucifers or the new French kind that used white phosphorus. He edged nearer, careful not to scrape his rifle or pistols. None of the other soldiers was anywhere near. He assumed they had all taken cover.

The duke growled in Wallanchian, evidently telling the pair to hurry up.

The man with the matches also produced a special abrasive sheet to strike them against and placed it flat between his legs. He selected a match, closed the container, and slipped the container back into the saddlebag.

Shakespeare wedged the Hawken to his right shoulder and curled back the hammer. He had an idea how to turn the tables and prayed to God his brainstorm worked.

A flick of his wrist, and the man holding the match ignited

it. Cupping his other hand to the flame so the breeze wouldn't extinguish it, he carefully applied the match to the end of the six-inch fuse. The fuse sputtered, then caught. Hissing like a snake, it spit coils of gray smoke.

Duke Alonzo gestured at the tunnel and snarled more commands. The second soldier, a broad-chested, muscular man, lifted the cask and stepped into the tunnel. His eyes were glued to the fuse. When it burned low, he would hurl the cask as far as he could.

Alonzo and the other soldier started to back off.

Shakespeare trained his Hawken on the muscular trooper's sternum, then concentrated on the fuse, like everyone else. He had to time his shot just right.

The duke vanished behind some boulders. A few gleaming helmets showed where some of his underlings were crouched.

The soldier holding the cask nervously licked his lips. He took a step and cocked his arms, getting ready to throw.

Shakespeare heard a rustling noise on his right and glanced at the opposite wall. Blue Water Woman was on her stomach, her rifle flush with her shoulder, grinning at him. "I thought I told you to stay put," Shakespeare whispered.

"Since when does a wife listen to her husband?" Blue Water Woman replied. "Besides, two rifles are better than one."

Shakespeare couldn't argue there. He was counting on his slug to knock the soldier backward, out of the tunnel. Two slugs would have twice the impact. "When I say to fire," he whispered.

Over half the fuse was gone. Some smoke drifted into the big soldier's face, and he coughed and blinked to clear his eyes.

Another ten seconds, Shakespeare guessed, taking a deep breath to steady his aim. When the man tensed and started to sweep the cask in an overhand arc, Shakespeare whispered, "Now!" and smoothly stroked the trigger. Blue Water Woman's shot and his sounded as one.

The soldier holding the cask was punched backward half a

dozen steps, dead on his feet. His lifeless husk swayed, then toppled, but instead of falling backward, he pitched forward onto his face. And the cask, instead of rolling toward the boulders, rolled forward, *into the tunnel*.

"Cover me!" Shakespeare surged upright and raced toward it. He left the Hawken on the ground and filled his left hand with a pistol. Shouts had broken out, and soldiers were rising from concealment. They hadn't seen him yet, but they would soon.

Only a few seconds remained. The fuse had burned to a stub and would set off the black powder at any instant.

Sunshine splashed Shakespeare as he took a final few bounds. A soldier hollered and brought a rifle to bear, and without breaking stride Shakespeare shot him through the cheek. Dropping the flintlock, Shakespeare gripped the cask in both hands. The fuse was almost gone. He raised the cask overhead and saw another soldier point a rifle at him. The crack of Blue Water Woman's pistol felled the man where he stood.

Other soldiers opened fire. Shakespeare was jarred by a shot to the right shoulder. How badly he was hit he couldn't say, but it almost made him drop the cask. Taking a long step, he swung both arms with all his strength.

The cask arced toward the boulders.

Shakespeare spun and flew into the tunnel as if his feet were endowed with the wings of Mercury. A glance back showed panicked soldiers fleeing every which way. A heartbeat later the cask struck the top of a boulder and split open, spilling a third of its powder at the exact moment the detonation took place.

Shakespeare hadn't intended for the cask to break. The ruptured seal and loss of powder meant less of an explosion, and he was hoping to wipe out half the Wallanchians in one fell swoop. Even diminished, the blast lifted him off his feet and flung him five or six yards. He spilled onto his side in the dirt, his wounded shoulder a wellspring of agony. Dust filled the tunnel, choking him, blinding him.

Then a groping hand found his, and Shakespeare was helped

onto his knees by Blue Water Woman. Her mouth brushed his ear. "I saw you hit. Can you make it on your own?"

"Just watch me. I could carry you if I had to," Shakespeare said. Which wasn't quite true. His shoulder was throbbing and a damp sensation was spreading down his back and across his chest. He was bleeding—bleeding a lot.

They ran inward, Shakespeare with a hand over his mouth and nose to keep from gagging on the dust. Out past the entrance a soldier shrieked in anguish. A few desultory shots were fired, but they struck the tunnel walls and ceiling.

The dust began to thin at the same second a tall figure loomed out of the gloom. "Halt! Who goes there?" Prince Ferdinand demanded.

"The Queen of England," Shakespeare grumped, and swatted the prince's rifle aside. "Watch where you're pointing that thing!" Stumbling to the pool, he sank down. Dust caked him from head to toe, and as he hiked at his buckskin shirt a shower of fine particles sprinkled to the ground. The movement provoked more torment.

Blue Water Woman joined him. Cradled in her right elbow was his rifle as well as hers, and she deposited his Hawken beside him, saying, "I thought you might need this."

Miranda saw the blood on Shakespeare's shirt and exclaimed, "Mr. McNair! You've been shot!"

"Thanks for telling me. I never would have known." Shakespeare was making light of his wound, but he had been lucky. The ball had entered below his collarbone, sheared through solid flesh, and exited above his shoulder blade. A fraction of an inch higher and his collarbone would have been shattered. A fraction of an inch lower and a major artery or vein would have been severed. Already the bleeding had dwindled dramatically. It was a shame he couldn't say the same about the pain.

"Is the duke still alive?" Prince Ferdinand asked the pertinent question.

As if in response, Duke Alonzo unleashed a string of Wallanchian invective, ending with a shorter but no less vehement assortment of curses and livid oaths in English, the ranting of a man driven to the brink of sheer and total rage. He concluded with "You will all die horrible, lingering deaths! Do you hear me? I have a six-inch sliver of stone in my leg, thanks to you! Now I will take you alive so I can torture each and every one of you until you beg for mercy! I will gut you and pull out your intestines! I will chop off your fingers and force them down your throats! I will cut out your tongues, drive stakes through your eyes!"

"He is a demon!" Miranda breathed.

"He's a jackass," Shakespeare amended. "If he was smart, he'd use the other cask of black powder."

Miranda fingered her rifle. "So what now? Do we wait for them to make the next move?"

"No," said a voice from low to the cavern floor. "You must carry the fight to them if you are to prevail."

Count Prospero had crawled clear around the pool with a heavy pistol in his hand and was now laboriously pulling himself up so he could sit on the rim. Miranda leaped to help, supporting him with both arms.

"They'll be waiting for us to try a stunt like that," Shakespeare commented. "We'd run right into their muzzles."

"Too bad the dust is already settling," Prince Ferdinand said. "They couldn't see us in that."

Blue Water Woman wore the same thoughtful expression she had earlier. "I have been thinking," she told Shakespeare. "We have two horses. And there is a lot of firewood stacked over against the wall."

"So?" the prince said.

Shakespeare grinned. "So all we need is rope and we can play 'fill the duke with lead.' " He looked at the count. "About twenty feet would do us if you have some handy."

Prospero nodded at the cabinets. "All the rope we have is stored there. Help yourselves to as much as you need."

Blue Water Woman nudged Miranda and the two women dashed off.

"What good will rope do us against guns?" Prince Ferdinand asked, perplexed. "Rope can't stop bullets."

"No, but it drags wood real good." Shakespeare cupped a hand in the pool and dribbled water onto the bullet hole. He winced as the cold sensation gave rise to goose bumps. "We'll tie firewood into two large bundles, one for each horse to pull. Then we'll light the wood. When the flames are nice and high, we'll throw a little water on the bundles to make a lot of smoke—"

"I understand!" Prince Ferdinand interrupted. "We'll send the horses out the tunnel ahead of us, and the soldiers won't be able to see us for all the smoke. We will be right on top of them before they fire a shot."

"That's the plan," Shakespeare confirmed. A plan fraught with more holes than a prairie-dog town. The Wallanchians might shoot the horses before the animals made it out of the tunnel. Or the soldiers might suspect what they were up to and unleash a volley when they emerged. But he saw no need to mention the drawbacks.

"Your wife thought of this? She has a shrewd mind," the younger man said.

"All females are shrewd," Shakespeare responded. "Some just like to pretend they're not so us males will feel like we have half a brain."

"Not Miranda. She is the most honest woman I have ever met." A tender hunger came into the prince's eyes. "My father sent me to find an embezzler and his daughter, and instead I have found the woman I intend to ask to be my bride and my future father-in-law."

"Really? Now, there's something I didn't expect."

Count Prospero was flabbergasted. "My daughter and you, Prince Ferdinand? But you've only just met again after all these years."

155

"Yet I feel as if my heart has always been hers," the heir apparent said.

At that juncture the women rushed back, Blue Water Woman bearing coils of rope, Miranda's arms burdened with firewood. Another trip was called for to get more, and the prince graciously offered to go with her.

Shakespeare cut the rope into twenty-foot lengths while Blue Water Woman stacked the dead limbs into roughly equal separate piles. Shakespeare looped one end of each rope around a bundle and knotted them tight. All that remained was to tie the other ends of the ropes to Snowcap and the roan.

"Fetch the lantern," Shakespeare instructed Miranda, but it was Prince Ferdinand who went to get it. Shakespeare splashed a last handful of water on his wound, clenched his teeth, and shrugged back into his buckskin shirt.

"You should let me bandage you," Blue Water Woman said.

"When this is over with," Shakespeare responded, rising. He wondered why it was they hadn't heard a peep out of the duke in a while, and moved to the tunnel. Shadows flitted at the far end. Barely audible whispering suggested the soldiers were up to something. "We'd best hurry," he advised the others.

"What can I do to help?" Count Prospero asked.

"Shoot any of the soldier boys who make it past us." Shakespeare accepted the lantern from the prince and walked past the horses. Snowcap was calm enough, but the explosion had agitated the roan and it kept stamping a front hoof and nickering. Kneeling between the bundles, Shakespeare opened the lantern, inserted a thin branch into the flame, and held it there a few seconds. He applied the burning brand to first one bundle, then the next, and soon both crackled with growing flames.

Blue Water Woman had brought over a bowl brimming with water. "I am ready when you are, husband."

Favoring his hurt shoulder, Shakespeare took hold of both sets of reins and led Snowcap and the roan to the tunnel. He rubbed the mare's neck one last time in case she didn't make it through alive, then retrieved his rifle and stepped to his wife's side. Miranda and the prince flanked her.

The bundles were fully on fire. If they waited any longer, the flames would burn through the ropes. Shakespeare nodded at Blue Water Woman, who bent and poured water onto each bundle. Loud hissing resulted and dense smoke spiraled toward the vaulted cavern roof.

"Shoot sharps the words," Shakespeare said. Stepping up to the horses, he gave the roan a sharp smack on the rump with his good arm, pivoted, and smacked Snowcap. Both galloped on down the tunnel, the pounding of their hoofs amplified tenfold. In their wake whipped the burning bundles, pouring thick white clouds.

"Now!" Shakespeare yelled, and led the rush. Already the tunnel brimmed with swirling smoke, and when he accidentally inhaled too deeply his lungs protested. He coughed, doubling over, but didn't stop running, not when every second was crucial. Mentally, he gauged the distance he covered, and just about the time he thought he should be hurtled from the tunnel into bright sunlight.

Blue Water Woman, Miranda, and Prince Ferdinand were only steps behind. The four of them raised their rifles, seeking targets, and as one they transformed to marble, making no attempt to shoot.

"Surprise, surprise," Duke Viktor Alonzo taunted.

Twelve grim-faced soldiers were arrayed in a semicircle, their rifles pointed and cocked. At their center stood the duke, a tourniquet on his left leg, a pistol in his right hand.

Shakespeare saw Snowcap and the roan trotting northward. They had angled to the right instead of plunging in among the Wallanchians and sowing confusion as he had hoped.

"Make no mistake," Duke Alonzo said. "One wrong move, one suspicious twitch, and my men have orders to kill you where you stand." A malicious grin creased his face. "I suggest you drop your weapons and enjoy a few more minutes of life."

Prince Ferdinand looked set to tear into them despite the odds. "I would rather die fighting than by being tortured to death! Do your worst! A prince of the realm never surrenders!"

"Oh?" Duke Alonzo bobbed his head at Miranda. "And what about the countess? Are you willing to deprive her of a few precious moments of life to satisfy your honor?"

"I will gladly die by his side!" Miranda answered for herself.

The duke's sneer dripped venom. "Such sickening righteousness! Such misguided devotion! The two of you make a perfect match. A match of morons. I am doing Wallanchia a favor by depriving my country of your obnoxious posturing." He pointed his pistol at Miranda's breast. "What will it be, Ariel? Do you value this wench more than your pride? Or do I squeeze the trigger?"

"Squeeze it!" Miranda challenged him.

"*No!*" The young prince blanched and lowered his rifle. "Spare her, Viktor. I beseech you."

The duke laughed, then motioned at two of his men, who promptly relieved Shakespeare and his companions of their rifles. Their pistols would be next.

Shakespeare fumed in helpless frustration, desperate for a means of gaining the upper hand.

Alonzo limped over to Miranda and raked her with a lecherous gaze. "What is it he sees in you, woman? How did he fall for you so quickly? Is it because you have the morals of a trollop from living as a primitive for so long? Did you let him taste your wares five minutes after he saw you?"

Miranda hit him. She hauled off and slapped him full across the cheek, her fingernails clawing his skin deep enough to draw blood.

The look that came over Duke Alonzo was hatred personified. Swearing, he struck her on the jaw, a solid punch that crumpled her to her hands and knees. "Damn you, bitch!" he spat. "For that I will save you for last and let my men indulge themselves!"

Shakespeare was watching Miranda and almost missed

glimpsing the enormous dark shape that reared up out of the undergrowth behind the Wallanchians. Kaliban had returned. Kaliban with his hood thrown back and his distorted features contorted in a fierce mask of unbridled fury. His fangs were bared, his cyclopean eye blazed with blood lust. A rumbling roar rose from his gorge, a roar louder than any Shakespeare ever heard, a roar that seemed to shake the ground under their feet.

The soldiers whirled as the hunchback waded in among them with a ferocity that had to be seen to be believed. His teeth ripped and rent. His steely sinews broke bodies as if they were rag dolls. Compelled by blind fear, the soldiers farthest from him opened fire, heedless of their comrades, and while some of their shots hit other Wallanchians, many scored, for Shakespeare saw the giant shudder.

Duke Alonzo had also spun and was gawking at the havoc being wrought. But only for another moment. Turning, he sprang past Miranda and into the tunnel, deserting those who had served him so well and so long.

Shakespeare didn't care about the duke. Drawing both pistols, he barreled into the melee, going to Kaliban's aid. He shot a trooper about to cut loose with a rifle, then sent a slug into another soldier stalking the hunchback from the rear. Blue Water Woman materialized at his elbow and dropped another. Prince Ferdinand, he saw, had wrapped an arm around Miranda and was pulling her to safety.

Not one soldier fired at them. Kaliban, and Kaliban alone, bore the brunt of the combat. He was a living whirlwind of destruction. One moment he snapped an adversary's neck, the next he sank his teeth into a jugular, and the next he lifted a squalling Wallanchian overhead and dashed the man against the boulders.

Suddenly the firing stopped, the yelling ceased. There was no one left to shoot, no one alive to cry out. Prone red uniforms were everywhere, some with arms or legs bent at impossible angles, some with throats torn wide. Bone gleamed in the sunlight. Blood pulsed scarlet.

Kaliban was still on his feet, but he teetered as he took a step toward Miranda. He had bullet holes in his chest, bullet holes in his arms, even a bullet hole above his right eye. Somehow he raised his hand. Somehow he moved his fingers in sign language. Then, soundlessly, he sank to earth, wheezed once, and was gone.

Miranda had recovered and ran to him. Gushing tears, she threw herself on his huge body, screaming, "No! No! No!" She ignored the prince, who tried to comfort her, and pressed her cheek to the hunchback's robe. "Did you see?" she gasped between sobs. "Did you see him? He signed that he was sorry he ran off. *He was sorry*—" Her voice broke, and she wailed uncontrollably.

A final shot sounded, from in the cavern. Shakespeare scooped up his Hawken and sped into the tunnel, his wife keeping step.

Duke Viktor Alonzo lay on his side, half his temple blown away. Nearby, propped against a boulder, was Count Stephen Prospero. "I've done it!" He wagged his smoking pistol. "The murderer of my father is dead! It's over at last!"

"Yes, it's over," Shakespeare said softly.

Prospero stiffened. "But what is that I hear? Why is my daughter crying? Has the prince been hurt?"

Blue Water Woman's voice was strained. "Kaliban is dead. He gave his life saving ours."

"Is that all? She'll get over him soon enough and we can get on with our lives. Wallanchia! Sweet Wallanchia! We're going home!"

Shakespeare looked at Blue Water Woman. Silently, they turned and went to collect the horses. Shoulder to shoulder they strode past the carnage the hunchback had wrought, and past the beautiful young woman weeping for the creature she alone had truly loved.

# WILDERNESS DOUBLE EDITION

## SAVE $$$!

*Savage Rendezvous* by David Thompson. In 1828, the Rocky Mountains are an immense, unsettled region through which few white men dare travel. Only courageous mountain men like Nathaniel King are willing to risk the unknown dangers for the freedom the wilderness offers. But while attending a rendezvous of trappers and fur traders, King's freedom is threatened when he is accused of murdering several men for their money. With the help of his friend Shakespeare McNair, Nate has to prove his innocence. For he has not cast off the fetters of society to spend the rest of his life behind bars.

*And in the same action-packed volume...*

*Blood Fury* by David Thompson. On a hunting trip, young Nathaniel King stumbles onto a disgraced Crow Indian. Attempting to regain his honor, Sitting Bear places himself and his family in great peril, for a war party of hostile Utes threatens to kill them all. When the savages wound Sitting Bear and kidnap his wife and daughter, Nathaniel has to rescue them or watch them perish. But despite his skill in tricking unfriendly Indians, King may have met an enemy he cannot outsmart.

__4208-8                                    $4.99 US/$5.99 CAN

**Dorchester Publishing Co., Inc.**
**P.O. Box 6640**
**Wayne, PA 19087-8640**

Please add $1.75 for shipping and handling for the first book and $.50 for each book thereafter. NY, NYC, and PA residents, please add appropriate sales tax. No cash, stamps, or C.O.D.s. All orders shipped within 6 weeks via postal service book rate. Canadian orders require $2.00 extra postage and must be paid in U.S. dollars through a U.S. banking facility.

Name_____
Address_____
City_____State_____Zip_____
I have enclosed $_____ in payment for the checked book(s).
Payment <u>must</u> accompany all orders. ❏ Please send a free catalog.

# WILDERNESS

## #24

# Mountain Madness

<--->

## David Thompson

When Nate King comes upon a pair of green would-be trappers from New York, he is only too glad to risk his life to save them from a Piegan war party. It is only after he takes them into his own cabin that he realizes they will repay his kindness...with betrayal. When the backshooters reveal their true colors, Nate knows he is in for a brutal battle—with the lives of his family hanging in the balance.

___4399-8                                   $3.99 US/$4.99 CAN

**Dorchester Publishing Co., Inc.**
**P.O. Box 6640**
**Wayne, PA 19087-8640**

Please add $1.75 for shipping and handling for the first book and $.50 for each book thereafter. NY, NYC, and PA residents, please add appropriate sales tax. No cash, stamps, or C.O.D.s. All orders shipped within 6 weeks via postal service book rate. Canadian orders require $2.00 extra postage and must be paid in U.S. dollars through a U.S. banking facility.

Name_____
Address_____
City_____State_____Zip_____
I have enclosed $_____ in payment for the checked book(s).
Payment <u>must</u> accompany all orders. ☐ Please send a free catalog.
    CHECK OUT OUR WEBSITE! www.dorchesterpub.com

# WILDERNESS

## #25
# FRONTIER MAYHEM

$\longleftrightarrow$

# David Thompson

The unforgiving wilderness of the Rocky Mountains forces a boy to grow up fast, so Nate King taught his son, Zach, how to survive the constant hazards and hardships—and he taught him well. With an Indian war party on the prowl and a marauding grizzly on the loose, young Zach is about to face the test of his life, with no room for failure. But there is one danger Nate hasn't prepared Zach for—a beautiful girl with blue eyes.

___4433-1 $3.99 US/$4.99 CAN

**Dorchester Publishing Co., Inc.**
**P.O. Box 6640**
**Wayne, PA 19087-8640**

Name_____

Address_____

City_____State_____Zip_____

I have enclosed $_____ in payment for the checked book(s).

Payment <u>must</u> accompany all orders. ☐ Please send a free catalog.

CHECK OUT OUR WEBSITE! www.dorchesterpub.com

# WILDERNESS
## BLOOD FEUD

⟵――――――――――――⟶

# David Thompson

The brutal wilderness of the Rocky Mountains can be deadly to those unaccustomed to its dangers. So when a clan of travelers from the hill country back East arrive at Nate King's part of the mountain, Nate is more than willing to lend a hand and show them some hospitality. He has no way of knowing that this clan is used to fighting—and killing—for what they want. And they want Nate's land for their own!

___4477-3 $3.99 US/$4.99 CAN

**Dorchester Publishing Co., Inc.**
**P.O. Box 6640**
**Wayne, PA 19087-8640**

Please add $1.75 for shipping and handling for the first book and $.50 for each book thereafter. NY, NYC, and PA residents, please add appropriate sales tax. No cash, stamps, or C.O.D.s. All orders shipped within 6 weeks via postal service book rate. Canadian orders require $2.00 extra postage and must be paid in U.S. dollars through a U.S. banking facility.

Name_____

Address_____

City_____State_____Zip_____

I have enclosed $_____ in payment for the checked book(s).

Payment <u>must</u> accompany all orders. ❑ Please send a free catalog.

CHECK OUT OUR WEBSITE! www.dorchesterpub.com

# WILDERNESS

# #27
# GOLD RAGE

# DAVID THOMPSON

Penniless old trapper Ben Frazier is just about ready to pack it all in when an Arapaho warrior takes pity on him and shows him where to find the elusive gold that white men value so greatly. His problems seem to be over, but then another band of trappers finds out about the gold and forces Ben to lead them to it. It's up to Zach King to save the old man, but can he survive a fight against a gang of gold-crazed mountain men?

___4519-2 $3.99 US/$4.99 CAN

# WILDERNESS

## #28
# The Quest
# David Thompson

Life in the brutal wilderness of the Rockies is never easy. Danger can appear from any direction. Whether it's in the form of hostile Indians, fierce animals, or the unforgiving elements, death can surprise any unwary frontiersman. That's why Nate King and his family have mastered the fine art of survival—and learned to provide help to their friends whenever necessary. So when one of Nate's neighbors shows up at his cabin more dead than alive, frantic with worry because his wife and child had been taken by Indians, Nate doesn't hesitate for a second. He knows what he has to do—he'll find his friend's family and bring them back safely. Or die trying.

___4572-9                                    $3.99 US/$4.99 CAN

**Dorchester Publishing Co., Inc.**
**P.O. Box 6640**
**Wayne, PA 19087-8640**

Please add $1.75 for shipping and handling for the first book and $.50 for each book thereafter. NY, NYC, and PA residents, please add appropriate sales tax. No cash, stamps, or C.O.D.s. All orders shipped within 6 weeks via postal service book rate. Canadian orders require $2.00 extra postage and must be paid in U.S. dollars through a U.S. banking facility.

Name_____

Address_____

City_____State_____Zip_____

I have enclosed $_____in payment for the checked book(s).

Payment <u>must</u> accompany all orders. ☐ Please send a free catalog.

**CHECK OUT OUR WEBSITE!** www.dorchesterpub.com

# WILDERNESS

## #31
# BLOOD KIN
# DAVID THOMPSON

Growing up in the wild frontier of the Rockies, Zach King survives countless dangers, from nature and from human predators. Like his father, the legendary Nate King, Zach has learned to anticipate threats before they appear. But even Zach can't predict the danger he'll face when he travels with his fiancée to meet her family in St. Louis. He knows they'll probably look down their noses at him because he's a half breed. He's used to that by now. But he doesn't know just how far his beloved's family will go to "protect" her from marrying Zach. Some of the self-righteous relatives will stop at nothing to save the family's good name . . . even murder.

\_\_\_4757-8                                   $3.99 US/$4.99 CAN

**Dorchester Publishing Co., Inc.**
**P.O. Box 6640**
**Wayne, PA 19087-8640**